GOLDEN ARMOUR

THE SHIELD

Up on deck, two scorpion-guards were contemplating the twins in the crow's nest. They tried shaking the mast to bring the children down. They tried leaping up, but they could not quite reach them. They hurled threats and missiles. They sent a crew member up to bring them down, but the twins shook the rope which he was climbing so hard he toppled off. None of these things succeeded in budging the twins, who clung to the crow's nest with grim determination.

Furious, a scorpion-guard seized a crew member and shouted at them, "Get down here now or I'll sting this man to death."

The twins looked at each other in dismay: they had no choice.

Also available in this series:

And coming soon:

GOLDEN ARMOUR

THE SHIELD

Richard Brown

Scholastic Children's Books,
Commonwealth House, 1–19 New Oxford Street,
London WC1A 1NU, UK
a division of Scholastic Ltd
London ~ New York ~ Toronto ~ Sydney ~ Auckland
Mexico City ~ New Delhi ~ Hong Kong

First published by Scholastic Ltd, 2000

ISBN 0 590 63777 0

Typeset by DP Photosetting, Aylesbury, Bucks.
Printed and bound in Great Britain by The Bath Press, Bath.

2 4 6 8 10 9 7 5 3 1

THE ORIGIN OF THE
GOLDEN ARMOUR

In the midst of a treacherous sea, there is a tiny island. It is temperate and beautiful all the year round. But no one lives there, for it is bewitched. At the heart of it is a ruined temple – and a broken paradise.

It is all that is left of a vast island which Citatha, the goddess of nature, once reigned over. The climate was sunny and calm, and nature was always in balance. The temple at the centre of the island was magnificent then. Statues and pictures of the goddess were everywhere in shrines and alcoves, groves and gardens. She wore flowers in her hair, a robe made of lilies and a cloak sewn with a hundred different leaves. Graceful, silver-haired cats slipped in and out of the temple columns, like the spirits of past priestesses.

And then, catastrophe! A huge volcano spewed up masses of ash and lava. Its force was so great, it split the island into four. Tidal-waves poured over the land and vast tracts of Citatha's world fell into the boiling sea.

When the air cleared, she saw there was nothing left but four distant islands, shrouded in ash and full of death. Only a fragment of her paradise remained, and in the ruins of her deserted temple she grieved for her lost world.

In time, North Island became cold and bleak, East Island a burning desert, West Island a land of fogs, and on South Island the rain made the land perpetually flooded.

In sorrow, Citatha dreamed a great dream. Out of her dream there stepped a suit of golden armour, etched with many glittering patterns.

Citatha entered the Golden Armour and infused it with her magic. She imbued it with Nature. Then she left it to do its destined work.

It rested in the deepest vault of the ruined temple. The Helmet shimmered with frost. The Shield hummed with a hot and scouring wind. The Spurs were shrouded in mist. And raindrops glittered on the scabbard of the Sword.

For centuries it has waited there in that deep and sacred vault. Parts of it have by mysterious means found their way to the islands. There, hidden by time, they await the coming of those who can release the magic within them.

Only then will Citatha's reign be restored. And only then will the four islands become like the paradise they once were, beautiful and calm.

CHAPTER 1

In the silence of the small hours, when the moon was already halfway to the sea's horizon, Lord Tancred's ship mysteriously lifted its anchor. It turned in the calm waters of the bay and sailed from the shores of Temple Island, where he and his twin children, Cassie and Keiron, had spent some unexpectedly happy days together. The goddess Citatha, a powerful but unseen presence on the little island, had chosen them to reunite the Golden Armour with its four missing pieces. They had disinterred the Helmet from a gruesome grave in the Chapel back home on North Island, and fought a fierce battle for it with Prince Badrur. Now Citatha was propelling the ship on unseen currents towards East Island where the Shield lay hidden.

Cassie tossed and turned in her bunk. She was dreaming: she was standing alone in the vault beneath the temple, the Golden Armour lying in front of her like a man in a coma, between life and death. The vault was filled with the voice of the goddess. "East Island is dying for lack of water," said the goddess. "It is burning up. There is no rain, and the water in the caverns beneath the earth is receding. The one spring on the island is controlled by Prince Badrur's mother..." The voice faded. The scene changed: she was in a palace. The face of an old woman, fierce and painted, loomed backwards and forwards in front of her, smiling, then hissing, then smiling again...

Keiron, her brother, was dreaming too. He was trekking across a desert; the sun beat on his body mercilessly; he felt as if he was slowly shrivelling up. He too heard the voice of the goddess. "Somewhere, beneath this burning sun," he heard her say, "the Golden Shield lies hidden. It alone can bring rain to this parched land. Many people have stumbled upon it over the centuries, not recognizing it for what it was. You are different. You must find it." Keiron trekked on. Suddenly the sand gave way at his feet and he was tumbling down, down, down. He landed in a huge and silent, sandy dome. As he lay, dazed, he felt creeping over him little creatures with cold-blooded feet...

Cassie woke with a shudder, Keiron with a cry on his lips.

"I was having a dreadful dream," she said, sitting up.

"Me too," said Keiron. "It was..."

Cassie held up her hand. "We're moving, aren't we?"

They rose wonderingly and clambered up on deck. The moon was now balanced on the horizon. A flock of white birds, perched on the rigging, cried raucously.

Lord Tancred was on the deck, looking puzzled. "The captain tells me," he said, "that the lifting of the anchor was nothing to do with him or his crew. The ship left the island of its own accord. They tried to stop it..." He shrugged, mystified, and peered down into the dark, glinting waters, as if that might provide the answer to the mystery.

The twins watched the ship cut through the waters, the crests of the waves silvered in the moonlight. Each thought of their dream. "This is Citatha's doing, isn't it, Father," Cassie said.

"She was impatient for us to leave," Keiron added. *He* didn't mind that they were on the move again, but he knew his sister would have liked more time on Temple Island. She had suffered more than he had on North Island in the great tussle with Badrur and his monsters, and over that peculiar business with the oversized Child; he could still see the strained look on her face.

Tancred, his white beard blowing in the breeze, looked at his children thoughtfully. "She is impatient for us to find the next piece of the Armour. We must not blame her for that." Then, seeing the look on their faces, he put his arms around them. "Come, do not look so serious. We've a few days' voyage ahead of us, and we're entering warmer climes too. Enjoy it. Whatever lies ahead of us, we'll face it together."

The moon sank beneath the horizon.

"Look," Keiron exclaimed, pointing at some dolphins curving in and out of the waves beside their ship. The playful beauty of the sleek creatures, the way they leapt in the air to catch their attention, had the effect of dissolving their anxieties. As the ship ploughed on, steady on a calm sea, the sense of a new adventure grew upon them, and with it a keen anticipation. After all, apart from their brief visit to the tiny Temple Island, this was the first time in their twelve years they had voyaged out from home or stepped on foreign soil.

Each day the climate grew hotter and drier. The twins enjoyed developing a deep, walnut tan – it was a new experience for them, having been brought up in such a cold, sunless climate – but as the ship approached East island, the heat became a little too intense and uncomfortable.

The island appeared as a dark smudge at first on the flashing waters, but soon stretched out along the sky-line. Low, sandy-coloured buildings and a few trees became visible, with many small ships bobbing on the coast. The twins' hearts were beating nervously. *This is it. We are here at last.*

The ship edged its way into the harbour. A ragged and impromptu welcome party gathered on the quay: ships seldom managed to navigate the treacherous rocks around the island and visitors were rare.

"They don't look dangerous," Tancred said. He had fretted all the time the ship had been in the power of the current, wondering what sort of reception awaited them. He focused a telescope on the crowd.

The twins felt him stiffen. "What is it?" they asked.

"Guards, I think," he murmured.

The guards were marching through the streets of the harbour town towards the quay. They were like giant scorpions with human faces, hideous and frightening. They had strong jaws and red eyes; over their heads and shoulders flowed manes of tiny scarlet tentacles. They moved rapidly on six legs, waving claw-like hands. Having read about such creatures, he knew they had deadly stings in their tails – and that they were in the service of the Queen.

"Can't we stop this ship?" Tancred called down in desperation to the captain. The captain shook his head helplessly.

Tancred turned to his children. "I'll go ahead in the boat," he said. "You stay here until I call for you." It was on the tip of his tongue to add, "And if I don't come back..." but he stopped himself just in time.

The twins watched their father row towards the harbour. They knew nothing yet of the scorpion-guards, but, reading the anxiety in their father's face, they felt very uneasy.

"I don't like the look of this," said Keiron.

"Nor I," said Cassie.

What are you thinking, Will? Keiron asked telepathically. He was talking to his little wooden manikin, who was sprawled half-hidden in his hair. Back in the days before they even had an inkling of their quest to find the Golden Armour, he had carved Will out of a piece of willow he had found in the woods. Cassie, with her miraculous gift for bringing creatures to life, had transformed him into a living being. Will had lived through all their trials and triumphs on North Island, and Keiron would be lost without him now.

I suggest you take a very long drink, said Will. *For there's an awful lot of thirst on that island – and soon you will feel it.*

Keiron took heed and went below to fill his water-bottle.

Cassie followed him, but she had other things on her mind. She unfolded a wolf-skin and stroked it unhappily. It had once belonged to Tara the wolf-girl, who had died at the hands of the monstrous Child, while trying to defend Cassie. Should she take the skin with her, as a comfort? She stroked it, and it made her feel calmer. In her mind's eye, the wolf-girl's almond-shaped eyes were watching her. Reluctantly she tucked the wolf-skin away: she sensed it would be safer if left on board.

Back on deck, Keiron handed her a tankard of water and gulped at his own. Will ran down his arm and leaned into the tankard to have his own sip. *We don't know when we'll get another one*, he said.

As Tancred's boat drew near the quay, the crowd grew more expectant. On his lap was the box which had once held the Golden Helmet; inside it he had put various items he thought might be useful as gifts or barter – fossils, polished stones, carvings, small books – but when he clambered on to the landing stage and held it up before him, all the crowd seemed interested in was water. "Water?" they said, jabbing at the box, a look of desperate hope in their eyes which puzzled him. When he shook his head, they scowled, muttered, or spat contemptuously at his feet. He opened the box, but no one seemed interested in its contents.

Behind him, several people jumped into the boat, pushing aside the two rowers. "Where is your water?" one of them demanded, and this was echoed by several others on the quay.

Tancred shook his head. He was beginning to

understand: here there was, it seemed, nothing more precious than water. The sun beat mercilessly on everyone's heads, their tongues felt dry and swollen: they all craved for water. There were barrels of it on the ship, which the crew had replenished from a spring on Temple Island; and he understood at once the vulnerable position they were in.

Tancred's two rowers pushed a path for him through the crowd towards some camels which they guessed were for hire. There might just be time to get away before the scorpion-guards arrived. But even as they were bartering with the women who tended the camels, the milling crowd on the quay suddenly dispersed with amazing silence and rapidity, as if a gust of wind had swept them from the scene. The camel women shinned up their animals and turned the great beasts away.

Swinging around the corner from the town came the posse of scorpion-guards Tancred had glimpsed earlier in his telescope. Moving swiftly and decisively on their six whirring legs, their pincer-like hands pointing directly at the three men, their red eyes casting reflected beams of malevolent light, they surrounded Tancred.

One of them demanded, "Do you carry water on your ship?"

Tancred shook his head. In a flash the scorpion-guard's pincer-like hands were within inches of his face and its tail was swishing back and forth.

"You smugglers," the scorpion-guard sneered, "do you think we are so stupid as to allow you to bring in water so brazenly?" It turned to the other scorpion-guards and said, "Row over to the ship. Bring back all the water you can."

"No!" Tancred demanded, finding his voice at last.

"On this island you do as we say," the scorpion-guard snapped.

"But I thought the Queen ruled this island."

There was a perceptible pause before the scorpion-guard answered, its voice slightly less insolent. "That is so. All things are ruled by her. She and us."

"Then you should know that you are insulting one of her most distinguished guests," said Tancred, drawing himself up. He guessed how things stood, and the indignation he felt at being treated so roughly was beginning to overcome his fear of these ugly creatures.

"Oh, and who might that be?" said the scorpion-guard with another sneer.

"I am Lord Tancred, ruler of North Island," he declared, raising his voice. Several scorpion-guards paused and looked at him with curiosity. The scorpion-guard who spoke waved its two antennae in the air as if feeling for the truth of this claim.

Tancred looked into the ugliest face he had ever seen, eyes that seemed permanently angry and a mane that writhed at every movement. He tried not to show his inward shudder.

"No matter who you are," the scorpion-guard hissed, "no one, but no one, is allowed to smuggle water into East Island. Got that?"

"Even if it is a gift for the Queen?" Tancred retorted icily.

The scorpion-guard laughed. "She has all the water she could want," he said. "What would she want with yours?"

Tancred watched in dismay as the boat, full of bristling scorpion-guards, rowed towards the ship and his children.

The twins had viewed all this through telescopes. There was something horribly nightmarish about the slow progress of the boat as it came nearer and nearer, packed with those hideous creatures.

"Get up the crow's nest," one of the crew advised them. "We'll try and fight them off." The twins climbed up the rope ladder to the crow's nest, their hearts beating with fear, anxiety for their father as sharp as a knife.

The boat was a stone's throw from the ship when one of the rowers shouted to the crew, who were massed on the deck with various weapons ready, "Don't try and fight them. They'll sting us all to death."

The crew talked heatedly amongst themselves; but when the scorpion-guards leapt on to the deck one at a time, revealing a great springing strength in their legs, a few ineffectual blows, some arrows, and the stunning of one crew member with a light sting, were enough to make the crew back off.

Half the scorpion-guards followed some of the crew down below decks to the barrels of water. The bung was taken out of one barrel and the crew were horrified to see the water gush out. Desperately, the crew stood in front of the other barrels, pleading that the water should be spared. It was not the scorpion-guards' intention that the crew should die – the Queen had not ordered this – so they contented themselves with sniffing each barrel to check their contents. "If you are caught bartering this..." one of them warned, and by way of finishing the sentence, all the scorpion-guards clacked their claws together, a sound so horrible the crew felt sick with fear.

Up on deck, two scorpion-guards were contemplating the twins in the crow's nest. They tried shaking the mast to bring the children down. They tried leaping up, but they could not quite reach them. They hurled threats and missiles. They sent a crew member up to bring them down, but the twins shook the rope which he was climbing so hard he toppled off. None of these things succeeded in budging the twins, who clung to the crow's nest with grim determination.

Furious, a scorpion-guard seized a crew member and shouted at them, "Get down here now or I'll sting this man to death."

The twins looked at each other in dismay: they had no choice.

Tancred was shoved on to one camel, the twins on another. The great beasts rose and swayed forward in the burning sun. What cool sea breezes there were soon gave way to an unrelenting heat. The harbour town through which they trekked, of low-slung sand-coloured buildings covered in a fine dust, shimmered in the rising heat. Tancred and his children poured with sweat and felt their skin, barely covered with the scant clothes they wore, prickle in the heat's intensity. Even Will, who had his own mysterious source of sap, was soon complaining.

But the twins' fear had somewhat abated since their abduction from the ship. On the quay, their father had explained that they were to be taken to the Queen, who ruled the island, and who, on knowing their identity, would surely treat them with more respect.

"But she's Badrur's mother," Keiron objected. "She can't be friends with us."

"I have a notion that they do not see eye to eye," his father replied. "I suspect when he came to North Island his mother had banished him, probably for some appalling crime. At least we can try to get her on our side." For the sake of the children, he tried to sound confident about this, but he was more than anxious about the reception they were to receive. She could just as easily clap them in jail, or send them away, or enslave them, or. . . But there was no point in worrying, he could do nothing about it.

The long, slow, and arduous trek that followed was, if nothing else, a good introduction to the island. The undulating dunes seemed endless; but here and there were oases of green life, each centred around a deep well heavily guarded by scorpion-guards. At night they camped in these oases, tormented by bloodsucking insects and the monotonous song of the cicadas.

Three weary days into the journey they were hit by a sandstorm. At first the air felt heavier than usual, then the sky grew dark and the desert seemed to hold its breath. The scorpion-guards crouched in a circle, curling their limbs and antennae inwards. The camels lowered themselves and closed their eyes.

Tancred and the twins were given no warning of the sandstorm; they barely had enough time to huddle together under a rug before the hiss of the storm was in their ears and hair. It was a disturbing experience. They were buffeted and rasped by the sand swirling around them; the roar of the wind was deafening; sand penetrated everywhere, making their eyes sting and their hair seem to crawl with insects. The rug offered little protection but they clung to it and to each other, full of terror at the thought that they might be swept away or be buried alive.

It was over as quickly as it came. They shook the sand from their hair and clothes, feeling bruised and scoured. Their eyes were sore and their limbs were shaking. As the storm receded, the world seemed chastened and uncannily still.

Parched, aching and weary, they came within sight of a low-lying walled city. It was a wonderful relief for Tancred and the twins; what delighted them even more than the prospect of civilized life again, of cool baths and water to drink, was the sight of the palm trees dotted among the buildings, waving their green heads above the flat, tawny buildings like a welcome. Will, who had curled himself into a tight ball days before to conserve his sap, uncoiled like a spring and jumped about in Keiron's hair. He yearned to bathe in water – as they all did.

They spurred their camels on; even the scorpion-guards, seemingly so indifferent to the heat, scuttled faster. They passed through a great sandstone arch into the city itself. It must have been siesta, for it was very quiet and sleepy in the heat: only a few people moved about slowly in the shade. Heads appeared out of windows and watched them curiously as they passed, but there was no fanfare. They travelled to the heart of the city without incident.

"I hope I never have to ride another camel in my life!" Cassie declared with heartfelt sincerity, her body stiff and aching.

"Never!" Keiron agreed, rubbing his numb backside.

A wall curved out of sight either side of them, punctuated by little watchtowers in which they could see scorpion-guards keeping watch. They were led to a high gate. A mass of trees and giant cacti loomed above the wall, and when the gate was opened, they stepped into a surprisingly beautiful, lush garden. There were great fans of glossy leaves, huge blooms of every hue, weird and fantastic cacti, immaculate carpets of grass, flowering creepers hanging like garlands. Gaudy parrots, bright canaries and other colourful birds squawked and flitted in the trees; snakes curled around branches; lizards basked on stones; beetles ambled through the undergrowth; and a lemur sprawled along a branch stared at them with bright brown eyes. After the scouring emptiness of the desert, this was like a vision; the twins and their father stood in a daze, drinking in the vibrant colours.

"This way," one of the scorpion-guards said, now noticeably politer, and he led them along a winding path through the garden for quite some way, until they came into a more formal garden where there were expanses of smooth grass and small cultivated flower-beds.

In the centre of these stood the Palace of the Fountains. It was a fantastic building, carved, or so it seemed, from huge blocks of sandstone; a forest of twisting spires and uneven battlements, crooked windows, and great carvings of cacti everywhere. Above the entrance to the palace was the biggest carving of all, showing a lizard writhing in a circle of flames.

But the twins hardly glanced at the building. What drew their attention was a fountain in the middle of the lawn directly in front of the Palace. Tall as a palm tree, it consisted of an arrangement of discs which reduced in size the higher they were set, creating a sort of cone. Down this structure flowed fountains of water, creating wonderful glittering sculptures in the air, and the sound of it was like music to the children, parched as they were almost beyond endurance these past few days. They could not help themselves: whatever the protocol of the place, nothing was going to stop them jumping into that fountain. They raced towards it, tore off their soiled clothes and plunged into its cascading coolness. Never had anything felt so delicious, so refreshing; they splashed around in it, wallowed in it, squealing like infants. They were dimly aware of the scorpion-guards jumping about and screeching in horror, and of their father beckoning to them to get out, but they needed this bath more than anything in the world, and they didn't care.

Will was having an extraordinary time too. He clung to Keiron's ear for some time, revelling in the water splashing all over him; but soon he lost his grip and went swirling away down a tunnel; then he shot up, propelled by a water-pump, to the top of the fountain. He burst out into the light and bounced down on the water from one disc to another, until reaching the bottom level he was snatched in mid-air by Keiron.

"Quick, put on your clothes," Tancred said, gesturing urgently towards the palace entrance. Scorpion-guards were lining up either side of the palace entrance and down the steps.

"The Queen is coming," one of their guards said, glancing furiously at the twins as they struggled, dripping, into their shorts and tattered shirts.

The Queen of East Island appeared in the great doorway. She caught sight of her visitors at once. As she swept down the steps, the phalanx of guards either side of her bowed low.

What an extraordinary sight she was! There was something saurian about her body, something turtle-like in its gravity, something snake-like in her movement. Her hair was a huge mound of stiff golden-grey tresses. She wore a long flowing gown of brilliant yellow, glittering with patterns of sequins that reached to her sandalled feet. She was tall and lithe, old yet seemingly ageless. The twins' high spirits evaporated as she bore down on them, and Lord Tancred had to remind himself that he was her equal in rank as he gave a polite bow. Her bony hands stretched out to them.

"Well, Lord Tancred," she began. Her voice was strong, full of vigour, used to command. "This is a tremendous surprise. I wonder what can have brought you here? And all by yourself except for your..." And she gestured vaguely, with a hint of distaste, at his children.

"Your majesty," Lord Tancred began. He was suddenly aware of how dusty and dishevelled he must look after the long journey. "I must apologize for not giving you prior warning. Our coming here was somewhat unexpected."

She flashed him an enquiring look.

"It's a long story," he said, bowing again. "And I hope you will..."

She interrupted with an impatient wave. "I shall hear about that in good time, I'm sure." She gestured towards the twins. "Your children – I take it these are your children? – had the best idea, did they not?" She gestured towards their wet clothes and damp hair. "You must come in at once and refresh yourself. The desert can be a cruel place to those who are not used to it." She turned with one movement of her snake-like body and led them towards the palace.

Tancred and the twins were puzzled by the matter-of-factness of this welcome. Relieved, too; it was not how they imagined it. But perhaps she did not yet know of their clash with her son, Prince Badrur, on North Island; her reception might have been very diffferent if she had.

"This is so good of you, at such short notice," Tancred said as they made their way towards the palace.

"Oh, but in truth I had advance warning of your coming," she said. "There is little that happens on this island that I don't soon hear about. Some of my scorpion-guards are allowed to retain their wings at birth, you see, and they brought news of your approach."

They climbed the steps into a vast hall. Cassie and Keiron tried not to look at the scorpion-guards flanking the steps, their bristling legs stuck out in regimentation, their red eyes glinting. Would they ever get used to such ugliness?

The hall was filled with huge plants, arching above their heads in a pattern of fans, filling the air with a heady perfume from a mass of blooms. Small fountains tinkled water among the plants. The Queen led them through a maze of dusky rooms and passages, pointing out features as she went – the books and scrolls in the Archives Room, the carvings on the wall in another room, the fountains gushing forth from sculptures of weird animals that reminded the visitors of the monsters on North Island.

They came to a great hall in the shape of a hexagon, with windows cut in every segment and a circle of light at its apex. Two thrones carved from blocks of sandstone were raised on a stepped stone plinth. There was a table made ready with food and drink, and a set of chairs. Otherwise, the vast hall was empty. That seemed strange to Tancred: no courtiers, no ministers? Did she run this kingdom herself?

"I am particularly interested to hear," the Queen said, "how you navigated the treacherous sea to get here, and of the purpose of your visit. But first you must eat and drink."

She motioned the visitors to sit and called for servants to hand around the refreshments. While Tancred and his children ate, the Queen sat on her throne and observed them in silence.

She is like an old, gnarled creeper, Will observed, keeping well hidden. *The sort that creeps round an unsuspecting tree and slowly chokes the life out of it.*

Keiron shot her an apprehensive glance and saw that she was observing him keenly. Her amber eyes were curiously bright.

"Your boy," she said to Tancred, breaking the oppressive silence. "The perfect age. Young enough not to be insolent. Old enough not to cling." She paused. "The last I heard from my own son was when he left for the Ice Castle on North Island. I take it he arrived?"

Cassie choked on the bread she was chewing – what a question!

"You find that amusing?" the Queen said, her lips smiling, her eyes sharp.

Cassie swallowed hard and blushed. "No," she said apologetically. "It's just that. . ."

"He arrived all right," Keiron said, coming to his sister's rescue.

Tancred waved a hand at Keiron to hush him.

"I see that my son has made an impression on your children," said the Queen, inquisitively.

Tancred was cautious. If he revealed that Prince Badrur was their greatest enemy, had tried to kill them and take over North Island, wouldn't she become their enemy too? Surely they must be in league? "He made an impression on us all," he said, hoping that would satisfy her.

But she was on the scent. "You need not be so tactful, Lord Tancred. I know my son. I know what he is capable of." She gave an exaggerated sigh. "He is wild, ambitious, selfish – ruthless, like his father before him, like most of his line. When he left here, ambition was burning in his cold breast. You look surprised! Prince Badrur was always my husband's son; his death was a cruel blow to the boy."

She paced back and forth before her throne. "I have fire in my veins, see," she said, thrusting out a bare arm and pointing at the raised veins, "but, by some quirk of nature, they had ice in theirs. My son has long since gone his own way. I am not responsible for what he does."

She paused before Lord Tancred. "I will not be surprised, my lord, if you have a treacherous tale to tell of my son, some black deed that he is responsible for. I will not be surprised if you are full of bitter complaint against him, and that your arduous journey here has been caused in some way by him. Let me reassure you, Prince Badrur and myself are like fire and water."

Her eyes were fierce with remembered conflicts.

"It is true," Tancred ventured. "He led the stone monsters against the Mansion on North Island..."

"The stone monsters?" She seemed puzzled.

"You have heard of them?"

She nodded slowly. "Is it not said that they were taken from here centuries ago, by one of Badrur's ancestors, to fight a battle on North Island, and were frozen there, petrified, as if into stone?"

Tancred nodded.

She smiled. "I thought that was just a story. Are you saying it is true?"

"It is, I'm afraid. I'm sure your son will tell you in time."

"And you say he brought them alive?" She turned and put her hand on the arm of her throne. "Why?"

Tancred wondered how much of the truth he should tell her. If she was truly disenchanted with her son, then might they be reasonably safe here?

"Ah, I see you hesitate, Lord Tancred." She glanced at the twins. "You have much to tell me, I'm sure. It can wait until you have eaten and rested."

She retreated to her throne. "I apologize for my son. He behaves abominably, he always has," she said. And then she added, a little archly, "I am glad that you do not extend your censure of him to me." She flashed an ingratiating smile, revealing teeth the colour of stained ivory.

Later, dressed in cool white robes the Queen had provided for them, Tancred cautioned his children to be circumspect in all they did and said. "It looks increasingly as if the Queen is on our side against her own son, but things are not always what they seem. Do as she says and keep out of mischief."

"Will you tell her about Citatha and the Shield?" Cassie asked.

"I shall judge what is best," he murmured. He had not yet got the measure of this extraordinary woman.

They were led back to the Queen's private apartments, a sequence of rooms full of arches and carvings and plants and animal-skins, with wall fountains trickling and blossoms floating in great pewter discs of water.

"While we talk," she said to Tancred, "I think we should let the children explore, don't you?"

She ushered the twins outside herself, the grip of her claw-like hands so strong on their wrists they felt almost bruised when she let go. "It is a long time since children were allowed to roam the Palace of the Fountains so freely," she observed as they emerged into a series of walled gardens at the back of the palace. "My son was never really a child, you know; he was always scheming and plotting and tormenting the animals with his hypnotic glare. You are lucky that you have each other; he only had his old aunt, Angharer, who nursed him."

"And you," Cassie murmured with a knowing smile.

She flashed the girl a warning look. "And where is he now?" she said ironically, gazing above their heads into the fierce blue of the sky.

"Sailing on a ship far away," said Cassie, trying to surpress the note of satisfaction in her voice but not really succeeding. For perhaps a second she felt the Queen shiver – with anger, perhaps, or fear, or maybe even love – but it passed so quickly she wondered if she had imagined it.

"We met Angharer," said Keiron. "She looked after him in the Ice Castle."

"Oh, you did? Well, I shall hear about that from your father, no doubt. Now, there are servants about, should you want anything," she said, taking her leave. "And some guards. Don't annoy them, they have a nasty sting." With a little chuckle, she turned and swept back into the palace.

In each walled garden there was a fountain made from discs graduated in size, like the one they had splashed in earlier. "Where does the water come from?" Keiron wondered, and they began to search in a desultory sort of way for its source, pausing frequently to admire some outlandish plant or try to coax a parrot to talk. They were aware of being watched from a distance by a scorpion-guard, which suppressed their natural high spirits, but they wandered down paths, through tunnels of leaves, under stone arches, over little ornamental streams and bridges, drawn on by the sound of a large amount of water cascading somewhere nearby. They came across gardeners who acknowledged them yet seemed curiously apprehensive of them and would not answer their questions.

"Perhaps they've been told not to," Keiron whispered.

They reached the outer wall and followed it around until they came to a great arch over a cascading stream. The stream fed into a dozen underground pipes. So this was the source of the water that made the Palace of the Fountains such an extraordinary oasis! They peered through the arch and were astonished to see scorpion-guards posted either side of the stream, which sloped upwards as far as the eye could see.

"The Queen's keeping the water all for herself," said Cassie in disgust.

Keiron gestured at the scorpion-guards. "I wonder why they do as she says."

"Perhaps it's like the queen bee – they feel they have to have one. She's the centre of their world."

It was twilight before they returned somewhat reluctantly to the palace. They wondered how their father had been getting on. They were shown by a servant to the Queen's apartments. She rose to greet them. They noticed at once that her attitude to them had changed. Now she was looking at them with something like admiration.

Their father was sitting in a high-backed chair by the fireplace. "I have told the Queen everything that happened on North Island," he said. "She is most unhappy about her son's conduct."

"Let us talk no more of him," she said dismissively. "Your father tells me you both have extraordinary powers." Her hands writhed in her lap as she spoke. "Perhaps one day you will give me a demonstration of them." Her face grew solemn. "And I will do all I can to help you find the Golden Shield. That, your father tells me, is why the goddess Citatha sent you here. I am honoured to be among her emissaries." And she bowed.

They felt embarrassed, Tancred because a Queen in her own land should never bow before another monarch or ruler, and the twins because they detected insincerity in her words.

The creeper twists and turns to secure its hold, remember, Will said to Keiron. The manikin had scampered about the gardens in great delight; but now, in the Queen's presence, he felt the air was dry and burning, and he wriggled deep into Keiron's thick flaxen-coloured hair, afraid.

CHAPTER 2

The twins were given a large room on the top floor of the palace. Its windows overlooked the garden. Two big telescopes had been placed one at the foot of each bed, trained to view the heavens through circular windows in the roof; and there were various gadgets, puzzles, books and drawing equipment on shelves and work-surfaces which they studied with mixed feelings.

"Looks like she thinks we're going to stay for a while," Keiron observed.

Cassie picked up a book containing legends about the Island before the Catastrophe, and she saw on the fly-leaf Prince Badrur's signature, obviously written when he had been a boy. She slung the book aside. "Do you think these were his once?" she said, waving her hand contemptuously at everything about them.

Keiron shrugged. "Can't think who else's."

He sat on his bed and focused the telescope. It magnified sundry stars, but becoming bored with that, he shifted the telescope and found that it could sweep the desert for miles beyond the city walls. "This is powerful," he murmured excitedly. "I can see a line of camels moving across the big red moon."

They amused themselves for some time scanning the dry, inhospitable world they found themselves in.

"Somewhere out there is the Golden Shield," said Cassie. "How on earth will we ever find it? It could be buried deep in the sand, far away in some desert."

"I found the Helmet with my telepathy," Keiron answered optimistically.

Cassie shot him a sceptical glance.

"Well, almost," he protested. "I can speak to things here too."

"That's what the Queen hopes you will do. *She* wants you to find it."

"So?"

"You're her blue-eyed boy," she teased. "You're everything her precious little Badrur never was."

Keiron curled his lip in a gesture of disgust.

"But when – if – we find the Shield, do you think she'll let us take it back to Temple Island?"

"We needn't tell her," Keiron grinned. He peered into his telescope again. "Look," he cried. A group of flying scorpion-guards passed briefly over the moon. "Don't they give you the shivers!"

Cassie refused to look; she was sick of the sight of the guards. She called his attention to Will who was swimming lazily in an ornamental disc of water among floating blossoms. "Have you asked what *he* thinks about the Queen?"

"Oh, he doesn't like her," Keiron answered, scooping up the manikin and putting him dripping in his hair. "And he no more knows where the Shield is than we do. Isn't that right, Will?"

You'll be led on a wild goose chase, said Will with a grin. *That I do know!*

Thanks. You're always so optimistic!

They got into – or rather on to – their beds, for it was too stifling at first for covers of any kind. The windows were open and the rustling, buzzing, whispering sounds of the garden mingling with the soft background hiss of the water from the fountains, filled their room, punctuated by strange bird-like screams which kept them wide-eyed for hours. The moon rose higher, the temperature dropped rapidly, and a cool breeze from the open windows stirred their mosquito nets. They fell into an uneasy sleep.

They were woken at dawn by a disturbance in the garden. Peering out of their windows, they saw a strange creature of a kind they had never seen before: it was half humanoid, half lizard. It appeared to have collapsed, panting, on the grass. Scorpion-guards were taunting it with kicks and blows. But the creature suddenly struggled up and spat with full force some fluid at his tormentors. It hit one of them on the lower part of their body, but although the scorpion-guard screeched and leapt aside, it seemed to have little effect. The scorpion-guards closed in on the creature, their two-pronged tails swishing angrily. One stung him; he writhed in pain, then he collapsed again and was still. They dragged his body away, chattering excitedly in their high-pitched buzzing voices.

Such an unfair contest horrified the twins.

"It was probably only looking for water," Keiron said bitterly.

"This is the Queen's doing," Cassie said, clenching her fists tightly, her eyes intense with anger. "I'm sure of it. Or at least she lets it happen. She's no different from her son, is she?"

Keiron nodded, equally horrified. "I hope we don't stay here long," he said. "This palace looks so beautiful, but. . ." and he gestured with a shudder to the place where they had just seen the helpless lizard-like creature being tormented and killed.

CHAPTER 3

"We saw a strange creature in the garden last night," Cassie said boldly to the Queen. They were sitting later that morning on a piazza before a table laden with all kinds of fruit, drink and bread. Servants surrounded them, waving big fans to ward off the insects and provide some relief from the already oppressive heat. Briefly, Cassie told her what they had seen.

"I'm sorry you should have witnessed that," the Queen answered, smoothing crumbs from her lap with slow, repetitive movements. "You did not sleep well, then?"

"It was too hot at first," said Keiron. "And then too cold. We're not used to it."

"Of course not. But I have sleeping draughts, should you ever need them."

The twins exchanged quick glances.

"Who was that creature," Cassie demanded, "and why did it have to die?"

"Cassie..." her father murmured, casting an apologetic look at the Queen.

She shrugged. "The child has a right to know, I suppose," she said. "They are the lizard-people."

"Ah, I have read about them," Tancred interrupted. "An ancient race; amphibious, I believe."

The Queen nodded. "They live in underground caverns where there are vestigial pools of water. We cannot flush them out, the tunnels are too vast and they are too cunning. They have a venom which. . ."

"But why should you want to flush them out?" Cassie asked indignantly. "Are they doing you any harm?"

Briefly, the Queen's eyes flared and her claw-like hands stiffened in her lap. She was not used to having to justify her actions, least of all to a child. "They lay claim to the Sacred Spring, child, which my family have guarded for generations," she explained in a hard, unforgiving voice. "Some silly, ancient tradition of theirs – which I repudiate, utterly." She glared at them. "If they ever succeed in taking the Sacred Spring from me, no one else on this island would stand a chance, believe me. We'd all die of thirst. Is that reason enough for you?"

It was on the tip of Cassie's tongue to say, "Haven't you just described what's happening here anyway?" She had seen enough to know that there was thirst everywhere in the city, and the people were suffering. But she saw her father flash a warning glance at her and she bit back her words.

"Never mind, child," the Queen added briskly. "You'll see many unpleasant things as you travel the island, I'm afraid. But after what your father tells me you have been through, I thought you would be hardened to that."

"Are we to travel the island, then?" Keiron asked of his father.

"If the Shield is not here in this palace, then of course we must."

"And the Shield is not here, I'm sure of that," the Queen chuckled. "Every room and vault in the palace has been searched, every spot in the garden dug over – it was done in my father's time, and in my husband's too. We are convinced it lies somewhere beyond these walls."

"Why were you so keen to find it?" Keiron wondered.

"It is believed," said his father, "that whoever has it controls the rainfall on the island. It has a magic as powerful as the Helmet, remember, although in a different way."

"The whole island could be like these gardens," the Queen cried suddenly, making a grand sweeping gesture with her arm. "No more deserts, no more sandstorms, no more fighting over the Sacred Spring. That's why the goddess sent you to find the Golden Shield. *And you must find it.*"

Cassie shuddered to hear her own ambition spoken by the Queen. "But how?" she wondered aloud.

"I understand your brother has a gift. He must ask every rock, every building, every grain of sand on this island if he has to, until they tell him." She looked approvingly at Keiron, who was wiping the sweat from his brow; he was beginning to understand that there might be some disadvantanges to his gift.

She turned to Lord Tancred. "But there is no great hurry. A few more days will not make any difference. You will need time to recover from your journey. Enjoy the palace while you can, while I make preparations for your search."

Lord Tancred spent most of his time checking back through accounts of previous searches for the Shield. He was content to sit in a pagoda being fanned by servants, trawling through great dusty tomes and drinking quantities of mildly intoxicating fruit drinks. The heat made him feel drowsy too, so that the twins often found him dozing, his book fallen from his lap.

Not that they minded. Keiron had begun to ask the trees, the stones at his feet, the walls, *Where is the Golden Shield?* He got nothing but a vague *It is somewhere in the sky* from the garden wall and *It is in disguise* from the stones in the path. The fountains spoke but their messages were obscured so much by the babble of the water he could not make them out. The trees protested that they were too young to know anything of so ancient a mystery.

By the end of a rather exhausting and disappointing first day, he and Cassie concluded somewhat hazily that the Shield was somewhere high up and looking nothing like itself, out in the great dusty expanse of the island. "At least we know it's not buried in the sand," said Keiron, reporting to his father that night. "That's something."

Doggedly, they spent the next few days exploring the huge gardens. Everywhere, a system of hidden pipes ran through the soil, and they could hear faint trickles of the water in the undergrowth. Shy, slow moving sloths and alert little lemurs allowed themselves to be coaxed down from the trees with fruit; gaudy, weird and long-legged insects were tracked and examined; flowers were dissected to see what they contained; cacti were split open and their sweet juices sipped; trees were climbed... But the heat at midday drove them indoors to swim in the basement pool, and in the hot afternoon they were allowed by the Queen to splash about in any of the fountains except the main one in front of the palace.

The twins were aware at times that the Queen watched them from a window or a balcony or from the roof itself, and at first it made them feel uneasy; but as she left them alone, they ceased to let it worry them.

One evening, after a swim in the pool, they decided to explore the basement quarters. Here little light filtered, the rooms were mostly empty, the shadows dark.

"You know," said Cassie, "it's very odd, but there's little trace of Badrur here, or anywhere, apart from the few things of his in our room. I mean, which rooms did he have?"

"Perhaps she's so angry with him, she's swept all his things away. He might have lived down here. I bet he never liked the sun."

"It never had any effect on him, remember? His skin was always white."

Most of the rooms in the palace did not have doors – they led from one to another through open arches, to allow such breezes as there were to pass through the palace, preventing stuffiness; so they were surprised when they came to a stout door on which was a repeat of the carving over the main entrance, of a lizard writhing in a circle of fire. The door was locked.

"Where could that lead?" Cassie wondered.

"Downwards, by the looks of it," Keiron said.

"Do you think there are deep vaults, then, underneath us?"

Keiron shrugged.

Let me look, Will said; and remembering another door and another lock similar to this one, he climbed into the lock and peered through the keyhole the other side. *Nothing but a tunnel*, he said, disappointed.

Later, they asked the Queen about the door. She narrowed her eyes slightly, then smiled. "Oh, it's just a store room, I expect."

"Don't you want to know what's in it?"

She shook her head. "I expect the key has been lost for half a century." She laughed, but they had the feeling it would be wise not to ask her about that door again.

Lord Tancred called his children into the Archives Room and showed them a large map of the island. They traced their route from the harbour where they had disembarked, from one oasis to another and through the desert to the main city and the palace. The coast was dotted with fishing communities; ruins of crumbling towns half buried in sand were marked; and the routes of wandering nomads meandered in dotted lines over expanses where there was nothing but desert. The Sacred Spring above the gardens was clearly drawn in too. There were two sites which particularly interested them: one was called the Lizard Caverns, the other the Lizard Ring. What were they?

"In some of the legends I've read," Lord Tancred said, "the lizard-people were the earliest inhabitants of this island; they probably lived at the same time as the monsters. What's left of their race now lives in vast connecting water caves under the sand. Here, I believe." He pointed to the Lizard Caverns. "I am not surprised the Queen feels threatened by them: their claim to the island is every bit as long as hers." He looked around him apprehensively, aware that he had spoken thoughts that he should more prudently have kept to himself. "But do not repeat this," he whispered. "Remember, we are only guests here."

He pointed to the sea on the far east of the island. It was shown as a swirling red eruption. "That is the undersea volcano that keeps the sea so warm and helps to make the island so hot. You'd be boiled alive if you tried to sail there. See, nothing lives down that side of the coast."

A few minutes later the Queen swept in, her long dress glittering in the sunlight. A red spot on each cheekbone, just visible beneath her brown leathery skin, was the only indication that she was disturbed about something.

She saw the map. "A few days ago," she said, her voice tense, "my son landed here." She pointed to a remote spot on the south-east coast.

Tancred drew back and looked at her with alarm. The twins held their breath.

"I did not tell you before because I did not wish to alarm you. I wanted to see what he would do. But now he has made his way directly to the city. And my guards bear out all that you have been telling me. He does not come alone."

"He has his monsters with him?"

She nodded. "Hideous things, by all accounts. But there are no more than twenty of them; the others must have perished at sea. My scorpion-guards should be able to deal with them if they have to. Come, we will be able to see his approach from the balcony above the main gate."

Prince Badrur's progress through the city to the Palace of the Fountains caused a sensation among its inhabitants. Few had any love for the prince, but they were astounded by his panting, salivating horde of monsters. They watched from rooftops as the procession passed, peering down at the monsters that shuffled along on four squat legs, drawing back in fear of the monsters that loomed high with long necks, shielding their heads as huge winged creatures with long savage jaws creaked by overhead.

At the head of the procession was the greatest creature of all, the Giant Salamander, who alone could speak telepathically to its master and to whom all the other monsters gave way. Insects were swarming about it and had settled in droves on its scaly skin, but apart from the incessant twitching of the ruff around its neck, it did not seem bothered by them. Badrur sat on the creature's thick neck, riding higher than all the rest, and when he saw his mother on the balcony, he waved ironically at her.

The procession came to a halt in front of the closed gates. Badrur was level with the Queen, the twins and Lord Tancred, and only a few feet from them. The sight of his enemies from North Island, there by the Queen's side, surprised him, and he looked to her for an explanation.

"Welcome back, son," said the Queen coldly. "You see I have distinguished guests. I believe you have met before."

Badrur gave a faint, grudging, scowling bow in their direction.

"You cannot bring those hideous monsters in here," the Queen said. "Why have you brought them with you at all?"

"They are my pets," he smiled. "I've brought them to amuse me."

"Keep them out of my way, and keep them under control. Otherwise, you know what might happen to them."

"Oh, I think they can defend themselves against the stings of your wretched guards, Mother," Badrur sneered. "These creatures once lived here centuries ago, before they were petrified by ice. Lord Tancred must have told you that. Think of it! I am bringing them back to their ancestral home. "

"You must know," said the Queen, gripping the wall in front of her, her eyes fiery, "that you are not welcome here. Not any more. I have heard what you did on North Island. You have disgraced me with the evil you have done."

"But this is my home!" the prince protested.

"Did you respect Lord Tancred's home on North Island?"

"Bah! So you prefer these *guests*..." he said it with such venom, the twins flinched, "...to your own family. Mother, you are growing soft in your sad old age."

"I cannot think why you have returned," his mother said. "Unless it is to show off these gruesome monsters. Are you thinking of becoming a zoo master?"

He laughed. The twins remembered that laugh. They both recalled a time when he and they were alone in a room in the Ice Palace on North Island, their lives dependent on his whim. He had laughed like that then.

"We shall not open the gates," said the Queen. "I'm sure you'd rather be in your caves. Your monsters will be happier there."

"Of course," he said. "I have no time to sit about a palace growing old and addled in the head, Mother. I am here, like your guests I suspect, to find the Golden Shield. You have heard that the Helmet was found? Well, the time has come for the Golden Armour to reveal itself, and I see no reason why it should be claimed by this lord and his two brats, do you? Our family is just as ancient and proud as theirs, perhaps more so."

He abruptly dug his heels into the neck of the Great Salamander. The beast, which had been watching the proceedings with its deep green eyes, turned to go. This set up a great commotion: the crowds that had gathered apprehensively to watch turned and ran, the monsters moved to follow the Salamander, and the scorpion-guards buzzed everywhere in an officious frenzy.

Those on the balcony watched in silence as the procession receded into the city.

"As a wild youth," the Queen said, when the din had died down, "he often preferred to live in cave dwellings several miles to the west of the city – they are actually ancient houses carved in the sandstone by a forgotten race. It suited me that he should be out of the way, for I could do nothing with him. And he would have taken over command of this island if his gift for hypnotizing creatures extended to the scorpion-guards. He has no power over them, nor much over the lizard-people: we do not know why, but it has been my salvation, and theirs too. Come, it is too dusty here, let us go back inside."

Lord Tancred visited his children in their room after supper.

"We cannot stay here much longer," he said. "With Badrur out there, looking for the Shield, things will be more dangerous, but we must begin our search too. Don't worry, the goddess will be watching over us, I am sure, and we shall be escorted by scorpion-guards who will have orders to carry out our wishes. It won't be easy, it may be long and tedious, and we shall all suffer from this heat, but you know we have no choice."

"Is this search a curse or an honour?" Cassie wondered aloud.

"Think about what you will need to take with you. We shall be leaving in two or three days at the most."

On the eve of their departure, the Queen visited them. They were finishing the last of their packing. She directed all her attention to Keiron.

"So much depends on you, child," she said coaxingly. "You and your gift. For I feel sure that only through you will the Shield be found. Persevere, and when you have found it, bring it back to us that we may share the good fortune it will bring with everyone on the island."

She laid her bony hands on his head and closed her eyes, as if willing her strength into his body, and when she left, Keiron stood there, looking a little dazed and starry-eyed. Cassie waved her hand in front of his gaze and then snapped her fingers at him. "Wake up, Keiron. She's only a bad dream."

Prince Badrur made rapid progress to the ancient cliff-dwellers' caves, and he settled his exhausted monsters there.

He felt no tiredness himself, and when nightfall came, he set off down a long, dark, winding underground tunnel that ran for many miles into the heart of the Palace of the Fountains. The island's ruling family had long had their escape routes to and from the palace, although in the last few generations they had not been needed; this tunnel, however, Badrur had made much use of.

He walked steadily for two days, pausing for rests, food and sleep when he had to.

Finally, he reached the door with the carving in the basement of the palace. All the way through the tunnel he had been brooding on the humiliations he had suffered at the instigation of Lord Tancred on North Island, and the fact that the Helmet had ultimately been snatched from his grasp. He searched out Tancred's room at once.

Tancred was lying beneath his mosquito net, muttering in his sleep. One slice of the dagger across the man's neck... He grasped the net.

"Badrur," came the Queen's voice behind him.

He swung round. She had not lost her ability to creep up silently and catch him unawares.

"He is more use to us alive than dead."

"How can that be?"

"He found the Helmet, didn't he?"

"*I found it*," Badrur hissed, outraged.

"Well, I'm sure we can use him and his remarkable brats to find the Shield for us. It's not as if we've had much success ourselves, is it?"

Slowly, scowling, Badrur sheathed his dagger. Much as he resented his mother's power, he knew she usually talked sense.

"Come," she said, and they went to her private quarters.

She sat in a window-seat and looked out into the night. "You dissembled well," she said approvingly. "They think you are as much my enemy as theirs."

He chuckled.

"But did you have to bring all those clumsy monsters with you?"

"Don't take against them, Mother. This is their ancestral home, after all. And a little display of my power won't do any harm among the rabble. I'm in full control of them."

"Just keep them out of my way."

"You are jealous of them, aren't you," he smiled, delighted at her discomfort. "Inside, you're just like them, cold and ancient."

"Enough of that, Badrur. I sent you away because of your excessive insolence, remember. I see your trials have not made you much wiser."

"Oh, but they have. I have learnt to use a little more of your cunning, Mother, and a little less brute force... But what do you intend to do about the Shield?"

"It is simple. When they find it, we take charge of it. You know that if it brings rain to the whole island our power will slip away. The people will not be dependent on us for their meagre supplies of water; and when that happens, the scorpion-guards will probably desert us too, or even take over."

"They would never do that," Badrur scoffed, thinking his mother was being deliberately alarmist.

"They only revere me because they think there is some mystical bond between me and the Sacred Spring," she hissed. "We *must* keep the Shield in our hands. I rely on you to help me make that so."

"I doubt I shall have the patience," Badrur said with a sceptical laugh. "It could take them a long time."

"In our family," the Queen said, leaning towards him, "your life is a vital link in a very long chain. Don't break it!"

They glared at each other, and then the prince looked away, a faint flush just discernible in his snow-white face.

"Tell me," she said. "What have you done with Angharer? You haven't left her in the Ice Palace, I trust?"

She was surprised by his reaction to that question. For a few seconds his face became like that of a sullen child.

"She fell overboard," he said in a grudging tone – almost, the Queen thought with amusement, as if she had chosen to leave him for something better.

"Fell?" she murmured.

"Yes, Mother. Fell!" he hissed, leaning forward, almost spitting the answer in her face.

She drew back with a smile.

"She was retching up over the side – she always got very seasick – when the ship must have lurched or something, and she must have fallen in."

"Couldn't one of your monsters have saved her?"

"I didn't see her go in and they are too stupid to know that she wasn't just going for a pleasant little swim."

"I'm sorry," she said, examining her long sharp fingernails.

"At least you needn't be jealous of her any more."

"Jealous!" she exclaimed in disgust, turning away from him. "You were like a changeling. I could do nothing with you, even if I wanted to, except curb your excesses. I was glad to hand you over to her."

They fell into an uneasy silence, each with their own thoughts and resentments.

A little later he said, holding finger and thumb an inch apart, "I was that far away from being the lord of North Island. I don't want to hang about here where you are the master. There are other islands I could conquer."

"There will be time enough for that. Now, tell me what *really* happened on North Island. I'm sure you'll tell a much better tale than Lord Tancred."

After several days of careful preparation, Lord Tancred and the twins were ready to leave. They each mounted a camel and made their way slowly through the main gate, watched outside by a curious crowd. Behind them porters pulled carts laden with supplies and tents. Scorpion-guards surrounded them, and guides went on ahead.

The twins wore wide-brimmed straw hats to provide some relief from the beating sun, and they waved straw fans in a vain attempt to keep cool. Water bottles hung from their saddles, but the water soon tasted stale and warm and scarcely had any effect on what felt like a permanent thirst. Flies and other insects incessantly buzzed around them.

It had been decided that, once free of the city, every half hour or so Keiron would alight from his camel and speak to the sand or an occasional rock. *Is the Golden Shield anywhere near this spot?*

But first they had to search the city. The caravan went from street to street, followed by a swelling crowd of excitable people, Keiron always asking for the whereabouts of the Shield. It took them five monotonous and weary days to cover every part of the city. The twins were all for giving up after the third day and moving on, but Lord Tancred, marking their progress methodically on a map, insisted they be thorough. "What if the Shield was right here, and we spent months looking for it in the deserts out there?" he said.

The twins struggled on, sleeping restlessly at night in little sandstone dwellings, being eaten alive by insects, aching from too much riding on camels, tired of their diet of camel's milk, dry bread and fruit.

But they learnt how much the people of the city feared the Queen and her scorpion-guards, and how much they relied upon the meagre supplies of water she allowed them at trading posts along the palace wall. Occasionally they noticed, too, among the city's inhabitants, small groups of shy lizard-people who kept to the shadows, and seemed more intent on watching what was going on than in participating in the life of the city. Certainly they were never seen bartering for water, and they melted away at the sight of scorpion-guards

At last Lord Tancred and the twins left the city, and struck out across the desert towards some ancient ruins marked upon the map.

Some nights later – a night like any other, cool and moonlit – they met Justus, the lizard-boy. He was to become their only real friend on the island.

The twins were roused from sleep in their tent by the sound of running feet and the high-pitched cry of the scorpion-guards. They peered out of their tent and saw, some distance away, a fierce commotion in the dunes. They crept forward to get a better look.

Suddenly, a group of lizard-people, caught spying on the caravan, broke free from the scorpion-guards attacking them and fled across the sands. A few of them paused long enough to spit venom: it seemed harmless when in contact with the scorpions' scales, but if it touched their eyes, then the guards screamed; some were screaming now. Incensed, those of the scorpion-guards who had wings took to the sky and dived on the fleeing lizard-people, felling several of them with their stings, scattering them in panic. Some of the lizard-people thudded past the twins, their tails and webbed feet scattering sand over them.

Lord Tancred ran to his children and stayed with them until the worst of the trouble was over. "Stay in your tent," he urged them as they stumbled back, rubbing the sand from their eyes. "You never know what dangers are out there."

They parted at their tent. Tancred went off to to reassure their guides and porters that there was nothing to fear.

The twins crawled back into their tent, their hearts still beating fast after the excitement. "I feel sorry for those lizard-people. . ." Cassie began. Then she gave a little scream. It was dark in the tent, and she could not at first see what she had touched – but it was cold, moist and alive.

"What's the matter?" Keiron cried. He pulled back the tent flap to let in some moonlight.

Between their two sleeping bags was a body – the body of a lizard-boy.

His large, brown, unseeing eyes caught the moonlight; his body, with its limbs curiously bent, appeared to have no life, but as the twins watched – the hackles rising on the back of their necks – they could just detect the faint sounds of breathing through gills at the side of the lizard-boy's very human-looking face.

"Shall I call Father?" Keiron whispered.

"Not yet," Cassie said. "Let's find out what's wrong with him."

"He's probably been stung."

They edged towards the lizard-boy, wondering if this might be some trick. Would he suddenly leap up and shoot venom into their eyes? Keiron wasn't sure, but Cassie sensed the boy's pain before she knew what was wrong.

Keiron lit an oil-lamp and held it above the lizard-boy. The light caught waving patterns of silver-green on the lizard-boy's back and tail and glistened on the pale yellow scales that ran down his chest and belly. "Look at his hands," Keiron murmured: they looked human, except there were claws instead of nails and webs of skin between his fingers.

"We'll have to turn him over," said Cassie. "To see what's wrong."

He was cool and slippery and heavier than he looked. They pushed him on to his side. "There!" exclaimed Cassie, pointing to a wound. "You were right. He was stung."

The lizard-boy groaned and his limbs twitched.

"Can you save him?" Keiron asked. She had saved countless lives during the battle for the Mansion on North Island, healing the wounded as they came in from the battlefield. "He is still alive."

Cassie put her hand on the lizard-boy's head. She sensed his life ebbing away. She had but a few minutes. She knelt beside him and placed her hands over the wound. The flesh was livid all around the jagged hole left by the sting and she was aware at once of the poison pouring into every vein of the lizard-boy's body; it was a miracle he wasn't already dead. She closed her eyes, placed her hands lightly on to the wound, and concentrated all her powers on that spot. All she felt was an outflowing of energy and a tingling in her hands. She was dimly aware of some battle beyond her vision, of two forces mingling and changing into something more powerful than both. And then the angry flesh subsided and turned back to green; and the wound suddenly knitted together. Lifting her hands, she saw no sign of the sting, not even a scar.

"I shall never understand how you do that," Keiron said quietly. He felt humbled by this gift of his sister's, it was so much greater than his own.

The lizard-boy shivered violently. He sat up. Now his eyes, dark and translucent, were alive with fear and doubt. He saw the twins and shrank back, hissing.

"Don't be afraid of us," said Cassie. "You were stung. You came into our tent to die. But I am a healer –" she held up her hands in explanation – "and I was able to save you."

Her words touched a half-memory and he looked, then felt, where the sting should have been. He was astounded at the smoothness of his skin. No wound. No sting. How could this be? He had a vision of Cassie drawing away the stinging pain, radiating coolness through the agony of his body.

He had survived the scorpion's sting! Such a thing was practically unheard of. No one but Tornius had ever survived a scorpion-guard's sting.

He flipped over on to all fours and wriggled slowly towards Cassie.

She did not flinch. She held out her hand to him. A long, thin, curling tongue darted out of the lizard-boy's wide mouth and touched the girl's hand.

"We are friends now?" Cassie asked, delighted, and the lizard-boy nodded. "Hold out your hand, Keiron, so that you can be friends too."

Gingerly, Keiron did so. He felt the cool moist tongue briefly touch the palm of his hand. It gave him a good feeling and he smiled.

Eh, what about me?

Keiron had forgotten about Will. "Oh, yes, and you must meet Will, too. He's a live twig."

Do you mind?

Will slid down Keiron's arm and on to his palm. The lizard-boy was startled; then his long tongue snaked out and curled around the manikin. In a second, Will was sitting in the lizard-boy's hand.

Help! Will cried, shivering.

Don't be such a baby, Keiron laughed.

The lizard-boy studied the manikin, then he smiled, amused at the way Will stood up and put his hands on his hips, trying to look fierce.

Not quite what I'm used to, said Will. *But his blood is more like sap than anything I've come across outside a tree.* He ran up the lizard-boy's arm and stood on his shoulder. *He'll do.*

And then the lizard-boy spoke. His voice was fluid and reedy, the syllables tending to run together like the flow of water, and they had to strain a little at first to understand what he was saying. "I crawled into this tent to die. I didn't want them to see me. And you saved me." He paused, considering the implications of that. "Now I have to stay with you."

"You do?" Keiron asked after a pause.

"If someone saves your life," said the lizard-boy, "you must stay with them as much as you can, to see that they are safe. That is our way."

"But you can't stay with us," said Cassie. "The scorpion-guards..."

"Do not worry about them: they won't attack me now. I have survived their sting, and they will think now that I am immune to it. Tornius, our leader, once survived a sting when he was young: they all thought he was dead, but just as they were burying him they saw his gills twitch. Anyone who survives a sting is..." He did not finish the sentence, as if something about it embarrassed him. He went on, "That's what marked him out from all the rest and why he was made our leader. The scorpion-guards are terrified of him, it's like bad magic to them. They'll never try to sting him again."

"Now they'll be afraid of you too!" Keiron exclaimed.

The lizard-boy's eyes glittered triumphantly.

"So, what would you like to do?" Cassie asked.

"To stay with you for now." He paused, slithered closer to them and said quietly, "You are on a great mission."

"You know about that, then?" Keiron asked.

"Tornius told us that you've come to search for the Golden Shield." He looked at them for confirmation, and they nodded. "We have been searching for it too. The Shield will bring rain. You believe that too?" They nodded again. "Our underground waters are slowly receding and we shall eventually die when they dry up."

"Can't you get water from the Queen like everyone else?"

"She would never give it to us. She wants to see us die out completely."

"But why?"

"Because the lizard-people are the true heirs of the island. Not her." The lizard-boy's tail twitched angrily.

"What is your name?" Cassie asked after a pause.

"Justus."

She reached out and took the lizard-boy's hand. It was cool and bony, yet in her grasp it felt curiously tender. "I'm Cassie."

Keiron took his other hand. "And I'm Keiron. We shall protect each other, yes?"

Justus lowered his heavy eyelids a little over his wide, brimming eyes: this was his way of signalling assent to anything that particularly pleased him.

Justus and the twins emerged from the tent the following morning to an angry, puzzled buzzing from the scorpion-guards. They were outraged to see a lizard-person among them and horrified to learn that he had survived a sting.

Tancred was as anxious as the twins that Justus be protected. He gathered the suspicious scorpion-guards together and said, "It is known by you all that a lizard-person who survives the scorpion sting is like a Chosen One among his own poeple. Justus here is such a one. I believe that he has been sent to us by the goddess Citatha – whom your mistress the Queen pays allegiance to, as we all do – to help us in a sacred quest to find the Golden Shield. Therefore, treat this lizard-boy with great respect."

The scorpion-guards buzzed together for some time, and then one of them spoke for all. "He shall be free of our stings. We do not harm those who survive our poison," they said.

One of them took off, to report the news to the Queen.

Justus by turns strode across the burning sands on all fours, his eyes always alert, his tongue flicking in and out, or rode on one of the camels with either Cassie or Keiron. From his earliest days, he said, he had been taken out with his people on the eternal hunt for the Golden Shield. It was a way of life for them, almost a ritual. He knew the route they were taking through the desert to the ruins, and the little oasis they stopped in to replenish water and food, and he did not hold out much hope of them ever finding the Shield. "We have been searching for it for centuries," he said. "Our underground caverns stretch for many miles under the sands, and we have burrowed in so many other places. Even with Keiron's gift..." and he shrugged.

Keiron's "gift" had become a curse to the boy. He was deeply weary of asking about the Shield, but the scorpion-guards watched him all the time and insisted that he do so, growing agitated and angry when at times he refused.

It took them nearly two weeks to reach the ruined city. It was a long two weeks. They were leaner, browner, more tired than they had ever been in their lives. But the desert had cast its spell over them – it had an austere beauty all its own and at night the cool dark sky was a brilliant dome of sprinkled stars which they never tired of studying.

As they drew near the ruined city, Justus shinned up a camel beside Cassie to catch a first glimpse of it. "I haven't seen it since I was a little lizard," he said. "My ancestors used to live there ages ago. It was our capital city, long before the Queen's city was built at the foot of the Sacred Spring."

He jabbered excitedly when the ruins finally came into sight, the remains of the buildings all but buried in the dunes; and then impatience got the better of him. He shot across the sand at incredible speed and was the first to arrive in the eerie city. Its sandstone buildings were half eaten away by wind, its windows were silted, its streets buried. Apart from the moaning of the wind, there were no signs of life.

In the centre of the ruins they found a dome, looking little more than a great mound of sand on the outside, but when Justus led the way through a little tunnel inside, it was relatively cool and empty. In the centre of the circular floor, which was covered with a thin carpet of undisturbed sand, were the remains of a well, raised on steps. "This was once the city's spring," said Justus. "Before it dried up."

They removed the wooden cover and peered down into the empty darkness.

"Look," said Lord Tancred, "there are some inscriptions. There, you can just see them." In the subdued light, they all craned to look, and they could just make out a ring of symbols carved into the stone. Tancred was excited by the find. "Justus, do you know what this says?"

Justus shook his head. "We did once have a written language," he said, "but it was lost when we were driven from the city, when most of us perished. Now we only use picture language."

This was like a challenge to Tancred and his eyes gleamed. "This then was written by one of your ancestors?" he said. "Maybe I can bring your language back to you. I wish I could get down there to see what it says."

"Father, you mustn't," Cassie said, putting a restraining hand on his arm.

Scorpion-guards had been peering into the well too, but they were impatient with this talk of lost languages. "Ask the well," they demanded of Keiron.

Keiron sighed. *Well, do you know where the Golden Shield is?*

Some distant cousin of ours may have it, came a deep voiced answer.

Can't you tell me more? He was tired of riddles.

No more, said the well.

Great help, said Keiron. He shook his head at the scorpion-guards. They buzzed and hissed their impatience, and Keiron got the feeling that they sometimes suspected him of concealing what he had been told.

It was decided that they would use the dome as a base from which to explore the ruins.

Once they had eaten and rested, the scorpion-guards insisted that Keiron should resume his search. "It's all right, Cass," he said when he saw her face drop. "You needn't come. Justus can keep me company. He's dying to go exploring, aren't you, Justus."

Keiron and Justus set off, leaving Cassie to rest in the cool shadows of the dome. A posse of scorpion-guards accompanied them.

Lord Tancred continued to peer down at the symbols in the well. Some he could make out, and these he copied into a notebook. But it bothered him terribly that he could not see what the missing symbols were.

Keiron and Justus trekked down the buried streets. Keiron moved slowly, for the heat was rising in waves, making the view before him constantly waver. He wore large, splayed sandshoes that gave him a purchase on the shifting sands and protected his feet from its burning heat, but progress was slow and sweat was pouring off him. The persistence of the scorpion-guards, always insisting that he ask this or that of the whereabouts of the Shield, was slowly driving him mad. Even so, the last thing he wanted was for the search to end in the way it did.

He was standing on a flat roof overlooking the rooftops when he heard, faintly on the wind, his sister calling his name. Peering against the sun, he saw her, no more than a tiny speck, floundering through the sand, waving frantically at him.

"I'll see what she wants," Justus said, and the lizard-boy scurried down the wall of the building and accelerated across the sand. Keiron watched him catch up with Cassie, saw them talk briefly, then part.

Justus raced back. "It's your father," he gasped. "He's had an accident."

"What do you mean?" Keiron asked. "Is he...? Is he all right?"

"She doesn't know. He's lying at the bottom of the well, in the dark, and he's not making a sound."

CHAPTER 4

Keiron tried to hurry through the shifting sands as best he could but his progress was slow.

"Jump on my back," said Justus.

Despite his anxieties, Keiron felt exhilarated to be sliding along the sand so swiftly, leaving the scorpion-guards scurrying behind, frantically trying to keep up.

"None of the guards will go down to him," Cassie shouted to him as he entered the dome. She held up a skein of rope she had found. "What shall we do?"

"Give me the rope," said Justus. "I'll go down to him."

"Are you sure...?" she cried as he perched on the lip of the well.

He slid fearlessly down the well's side, his claws gripping the rough brickwork. Lord Tancred was crumpled and comatose at the bottom, his fall fortunately cushioned by sand. With some difficulty, Justus laced the rope about Tancred's body, and he then called out, "You can pull him up now."

The scorpion-guards joined in and together they were able to raise Tancred from the well.

Cassie gently slapped his face and called his name,

but he did not stir. She felt over his body. "I think he's broken some ribs," she said; and a little later, "His left leg, too."

"You can cure that, though, can't you?" Keiron said, alarmed by the deathly pallor of his father's face.

She nodded. She laid her hands on his lacerated skin and felt the familiar tingling, healing power flow from her fingertips into his body. She could feel his damaged bones knit and she saw the broken skin heal over.

But she could not bring him round. A blow on the head had rendered him unconscious. Cassie found the break in his scalp and healed it, but try as she might, she could not rouse him.

"Let him sleep," the captain of the scorpion-guards ordered, impatiently. "He will come round in time."

The twins kept vigil by his bedside for half the night and for the rest of the following day. He breathed regularly but did not come round.

"I hope it's not a coma," Keiron said, voicing his fears. "They can last for an age, can't they?"

The scorpion-guards grew angry with Keiron for refusing to continue the search for the Shield. "How can I," he shouted at them when they pressed him too hard, "when my father lies sick?" It was an understandable outburst, and Cassie silently applauded it.

But when the second morning dawned, they deeply regretted it. Their father was no longer there. The scorpion-guards had spirited him away during the night.

"You would not search," the captain said, "because of your father. So we removed him."

Keiron was aghast. Nothing had prepared them for this catastrophe. "Where have you taken him?" he demanded, white-faced.

"Back to the palace. He will be well taken care of there. Now, boy, begin the search as soon as you have eaten. We have wasted enough time already."

The twins looked with despair at the rug that had served for their father's bed. You are on your own now, it seemed to say, at the mercy of a bunch of ugly, hostile scorpion-guards, with only Justus as your friend. Without their quiet, kind, courageous father, they felt lost and defenceless.

By the rug was Lord Tancred's notebook. Keiron picked it up and looked at the symbols he had copied into it.

You should copy all of them down, Will said suddenly.

Why?

I don't know. But the symbols describe a complete circle around the well. Circles should never be broken. It's like the rings in the trunks of trees – each has its own story to tell. Send Justus down to tell you what the missing symbols say.

Which is what he did, much to the annoyance of the scorpion-guards, who were impatient to get on with the search for the Shield.

At the Cave Dwellings Prince Badrur was getting bored. He had amused himself scaring the city's inhabitants with his monsters. He had listened with interest to the winged scorpion-guards that brought news of the twins' progress. He had spent time restocking the caves with dried food and making them habitable again after his long absence. But he was growing impatient. When he heard of the lizard-people's "attack", as it was described, on the camp, he was incensed, and he vowed once again that somehow he would wipe them out for good.

One shadowy anxiety still haunted him. The monstrous Child. He had heard that she had taken to the sea from North Island; hopefully, she had perished in the waves. In his nightmares she bore down on him, crashing through the city with her dark, blank eyes, her pudgy hands held out to seize him, and he felt himself in imminent danger of being crushed to death in a gurgling hug. He cursed the day when he had first set eyes on her, in the village where she had been born, where Cassie had brought her back from the dead. It was then that she had first fastened her dark affections on him, recognizing a kindred spirit. "Oh, let her be drowned," he'd cry out in the night. He had sent out flying monsters to patrol the coast. So far, they had seen nothing of her.

Then came news of Lord Tancred's accident. It seemed to him like a sign that he should get involved: this inactivity, and the boredom of it, was killing him.

He met his mother in the throne room. She was sitting on her throne, staring into space, feeding off daydreams and long serpentine memories. Where now there was only the sound of scared and scurrying scorpion-guards and servants, there had once been throngs of people paying allegiance to her husband. She had long and bitterly suspected the cause of his death – had it not been poison rather than the failure of his heart? Plotters and enemies were everywhere. She'd had no choice but to call the scorpion-guards into the palace to protect her. Now, with everyone having fallen under her suspicion at one time or another over the long, proud, lonely years of her reign, her throne room was empty.

"Mother, you've heard the news about Tancred?"

She inclined her head slightly, slowly blinking her heavy eyelids. "Of course. He's being brought back here. It'll be an incentive for his son to continue the search for the Shield, don't you think?"

Basdrur laughed his approval. "You're much too soft on them, Mother."

"Sometimes it pays to tread softly, Badrur. That's something you ought to learn."

"What if the boy gives up? They say he's getting tired and truculent. Without his father, he might. He's been weeks in the desert without success. How will treading softly help then?"

She smiled ironically at him. "Why this sudden concern for the boy, Badrur? It's not like you."

He gestured impatiently. "You also know, I suppose, that they now have a lizard-boy travelling with them? Doesn't that worry you?"

A shadow passed over her face. "The child Cassie saved him from a sting. That is inconvenient. The scorpion-guards will be sentimental about him now. But he's of little account. What can one lizard-boy do against us?" She chuckled dryly.

Badrur strode up the steps and sat on his late father's throne. Leaning towards his mother and looking into her suspicious eyes, he said, "We may not see eye to eye on everything, Mother, but in this we are one.

Keiron could find the Shield at any time. He is searching the ruined city now – it might be there. Do you think he'll meekly bring it back to us when he finds it? If he is in league with the lizard-people..."

"Of course he will," she retorted with a self-satisfied smile. "As long as he knows that his father is in our tender care."

Badrur nodded approvingly. "Even so, I think I should be there when he finds it."

"Ah, so that's what all this is about!"

"I am bored, Mother. I have nothing to do but look after those creatures, and all of them are dumb, even the Great Salamander. All they want to do is bask in the sun, gorge themselves, mate and lay eggs. Well, Mother, I am not a zoo keeper, as it once amused you to suggest."

The Queen found this last observation so funny she laughed – it was a curious wheezy rasping sound like two rocks grinding together.

Badrur hated being made fun of, especially by his mother. He leapt off the throne. "Well, you may sit here dreaming like an old woman," he declared contemptuously, "but I'm going out there."

She stopped laughing and regarded him coolly.

"You want to try its magic for yourself, to be the first. Is that it?"

He shrugged.

"But you don't know what its magic is. It won't be like the Golden Helmet, that magnified what was in your heart. And I thank Citatha for that at least."

"It'll bring rain, Mother. Water! However its magic works, one of us should be there to seize it." He spoke now as if he were talking to a simpleton.

She rose from her throne. "Go, then, if you wish," she said, her face darkening. "Not that you need my permission. But be warned, the scorpion-guards owe their loyalty to me, not to you, and the minute you part company with me they will fall on you and sting you to death."

She swept out of the great hall, her golden, sequinned dress trailing behind her.

The ruined city yielded nothing. The twins were feeling depressed, dehydrated, sore and resentful, and when the captain of the scorpion-guards demanded that they move on, they stubbornly refused. They leaned against the well in the dome, scowling.

The captain did not argue with them, but when new supplies of water and food were brought in by the flying scorpions from the nearest oasis, they found their share was severely rationed. There was barely enough water to wet their mouths and none for washing; and the slivers of fruit, meat and bread they were given were tiny. They indignantly demanded more, but were met with indifference. They appealed to Justus to help them, and he pleaded with the scorpion-guards. He succeeded only in getting a little more water.

"We'll have to go on," Keiron sighed, pulling his father's map towards him.

"They'd never dare do this if Father was here," Cassie muttered.

Lord Tancred had already marked a route on the map. Their next destination was called the Lizard Ring. A circle of rocks had been drawn around the name.

"Justus," Keiron asked. "Do you know anything about this place?"

Justus looked to where Keiron's finger was pointing on the map, and then he drew back sharply, shaking his head. "You should not go there," he said, looking around to see if they were being overheard.

"There is nothing else ahead but desert," said Keiron reasonably.

Justus paced up and down, his head bowed, until Cassie took hold of his arm and said, "Why shouldn't we go to the Lizard Ring?"

"If you go there," he answered with reluctance, "you should pass straight by it and go on to the coast. No searching. No digging." He seemed shocked by the thought of digging, and he said, "Above all, not that."

"But why?"

"It is a secret. We are taught as children never to reveal it."

"But if you don't..."

"Please, don't press me," Justus said in a sorrowful voice, and he slid away from the twins.

"What was all that about?" Keiron wondered.

"Shouldn't we do as he says?" Cassie asked. "It might be a sacred burial ground or something."

"Let's see when we get there," said Keiron, puzzled.

In the hot and unremitting days ahead, three separate parties made their way across the burning sands to the Lizard Ring.

The twins rode on their camels. They had rigged up makeshift shades above them to keep off the worst of the sun, and they fanned themselves incessantly with great wicker fans. Their bodies, thinner now, wiry and deeply tanned, had adjusted to the fierce climate; it made them tired and irritable, it hurt their eyes all the time, it plagued them with little flies, it whirled periodic sandstorms around them, covering every part of their bodies with gritty, irritating sand, but they endured it as best they could. At night, Cassie would run her soothing hands over her own and her brother's skin, healing the bites and soreness, the aches and itches, and perhaps this alone made it all just bearable.

The second party, which paused for a rest in the ruined city, had no such problems. Lizard-people did not suffer in the same way; their scaly skins were tough and retained the body's moisture, and they travelled best at night when the desert was cold. But being amphibious, they were always plagued by the *desire* for water, and yearned for their cool underwater pools; when the desire became too strong to resist, they searched the desert for hidden underground springs. The island still had them, deep and inaccessible in the sand. With their acute sensitivity to water, the lizard-people could divine where they were; but it was hard work digging down so deep, and they only did it when they had to. Now a large party of them were resting in the dome. Their intention was to rescue Justus. He had survived a scorpion-sting: this, being so rare, marked him out as a possible future leader. He had to be brought back to his people in the Lizard Caverns at whatever cost.

The third party also travelled by night. The silhouette of Prince Badrur riding high on the neck of the Great Salamander, surrounded by a motley collection of cold-blooded monsters, scampering and flying scorpion-guards and huge slowly flapping leathery birds, could be seen cut dark against the blood-red moon.

The Lizard Ring came into sight: a large circle of jagged rocks, like a set of decayed giant's teeth, looming out of the sand. Justus slithered ahead, moving over the sand like a streak of green lightning, so keen was he to be the first; and when the twins climbed off their camels at the ring's edge, they found him in the middle of it, his head to the sand as if he was listening for something. But he would not explain his behaviour.

"We will camp here," said the captain of the scorpion-guards. "Boy, ask."

Keiron scowled and pointedly did not "ask" at once. He was fed up with being ordered about by scorpion-guard, and he had grown to hate the question he always had to ask.

"Look at this," said Cassie, calling him over to one of the rocks. She was tracing her finger over an etching of a lizard. "They're everywhere," she said as Keiron joined her. "Look." The rock – and all the others too, as they soon discovered – was covered with drawings scratched expertly into the surface. The pictures showed every aspect of lizard life: hatching, growing, learning, eating, mating, aging, dying. "You see," said Cassie, "it *is* like a sort of burial ground."

Justus slithered up to them and rose on his hind legs. "This place is sacred to the lizard-people," he said urgently. He was agitated. "It must not be disturbed." He turned to Keiron. "Have you asked yet?" he whispered apprehensively.

Keiron shook his head. "They've told me to – but not yet." He moved closer to Justus and whispered, "Besides, it'd be a waste of time. We know it's somewhere up high, not in the ground."

"Then tell them that. Don't let them dig here."

"I've tried telling them. They won't believe me. They think it's just a way to get out of asking."

"Then leave it as late as you can," Justus pleaded.

"Why? What difference does it make?"

Lizard-people can sense the presence of other lizard-people for miles around, and lately Justus had been picking up signals indicating that his people were approaching. If things could be delayed... "I cannot bear to think of this place being dug over by these wretched guards," he said.

"We understand," said Cassie. "At least, I think we do."

They went from one rock to another. Justus explained some of the drawings, others he passed over. "Here is our history," he declared. "In the early days, my people gathered here from all over the island to celebrate. We told stories, we danced and ate and held ceremonies. It was a magical place."

"It still is, in a way," Cassie observed.

"But you haven't told us why this place is so important to you now," said Keiron.

"One day I will tell you," was all Justus would say.

At twilight, with the moon rising and the temperature falling, the captain of the scorpion-guards came to their tent and demanded that Keiron ask for the Shield. Supper would be denied them if he didn't.

Wearily, Keiron obliged. With Cassie and Justus by his side, and the captain watching him, he went from one rock to another asking the same question: *Do you know the whereabouts of the Golden Shield?* Sometimes he would vary it: *Is the Golden Shield here?* But the answer, as the three of them knew, was always no, which made the activity so pointless. Justus remained nervous: what if they didn't believe Keiron?

"Now the sand," the captain demanded. He felt sure that something was hidden here, and if the rocks would not reveal it, the sand might. So Keiron had to crouch on the sand, scoop up handfuls of it and ask the same questions. That made Justus even more jumpy.

The fateful hour was upon all three parties. Badrur arrived with his monstrous group from one side of the Ring, and the lizard-people arrived on the other side a few minutes later.

Badrur did not hesitate. He marched into the circle of rocks on the Giant Salamander, his creatures following behind. Reptilian birds and flying scorpions descended into the Ring around him. He dismounted and the scorpion-guards bowed.

The twins were greatly disturbed at his sudden appearance. And the sight of the monsters looming about them in the moonlight, their scales glinting, their claws tossing up the sand, their wings and fins and ruffs swaying menacingly, brought flashbacks of the terrible battle they had fought with these monsters on their home island, of the blood spilled, the flesh gashed, the cries of pain, the mounds of the dead. But they stood their ground; they had learnt that nothing was gained by showing fear to such a man or his monsters.

"Why have you come here?" Cassie demanded.

Badrur chuckled. "Ever the hot-head, Cassie," he teased. "I was curious to see why you have had no success. And my monsters needed a little outing, they are growing fat and lazy, don't you think. Come, surely you are pleased to see me?" He laughed sardonically and the laughter echoed across the sands.

"The boy has never ceased to ask for the Shield," the captain of the scorpion-guards said nervously.

"Yes, but is he always telling the truth?" He stepped forward and seized hold of Keiron's chin. "Well, my boy, I know how cunning you can be. Are you?"

Keiron tore himself free and snarled, "I want to find it as much as you. Why should I lie?"

"A ship that floats in a golden tunnel?" He chuckled knowingly. "You are in league with powerful forces, boy. How should I know to whose tune you dance?"

"Well, I haven't found it, and there's nothing you can do about that." Keiron's lip trembled defiantly.

Badrur brushed him aside and glanced around him. "I know this place," he said. "Sacred to the lizard-people, I believe. This is just the sort of place the Shield would be buried, don't you think?"

"I've already asked..." Keiron began; but Justus suddenly reared up before Badrur, his great green eyes glaring, his tail thumping on the sand. He shouted, "It is not here. Keiron has asked. It is not here."

"Ah," said Badrur, his eyes gleaming. "The lizard-boy. I have heard about you. You survived a scorpion-sting, I'm told." He turned to the scorpion-guard. "Why was this lizard-boy allowed to accompany the search? Why wasn't he killed?"

"I think you know why," the scorpion-guard murmured, embarrassed. "He survived the sting..."

"And that of course makes him untouchable in your eyes. Pah! I don't believe in such nonsense. Lizard-people are our enemies. There can be no accommodation with them. He will have to die. Seize him."

But the scorpion-guards clacked their claws and retreated, clearly disturbed.

In a fury, Badrur turned to his monsters and shouted again, "Seize him."

Justus turned this way and that, looking for a way of escape, but monsters were advancing on him, and he felt nothing but fear. He froze.

The twins tried to close in to protect him, but scorpion-guards intervened. They watched helplessly, their hearts beating wildly, as a flying monster reached towards a petrified Justus with a great claw.

Another few seconds and it would have been too late. The lizard-people hiding at the rim of the circle had seen in a flash what was happening. With one concerted movement, they streamed across the sand at lightning speed, the moonlight glinting on their cold green bodies.

There was pandemonium. The scorpion-guards, caught by surprise, flew or scattered, hissing in alarm. The monsters swayed and stamped about in confusion, snapping and clawing at everything that moved, waving their wings and fins in a frenzy.

Cassie shrieked and crouched down, shielding her head with her hands.

Badrur lunged forward and grabbed Keiron. He pinned his arm behind his back and called to his salamander.

Justus tried to snatch Keiron back but was dealt a fierce blow which sent him sprawling in the sand. He was about to be trampled on by a squat monster with large plate-like feet, when he was surrounded by lizard-people. Some of them spat venom into the eyes of the monsters and scorpion-guards; others seized hold of Justus and lifted him out of danger.

"Save Cassie," he shouted to them. "Save the girl."

Cassie felt herself being lifted by cold hands, but she was too terrified to look to see what was happening to her.

Within a few minutes several lizard-people lay wounded or dead, monsters bellowed and screeched at the pain from the venom in their eyes, scorpion-guards lay crushed and helpless while others flapped about in the sky in terror. Badrur was back on the neck of his Great Salamander, clasping Keiron tightly to him, and Cassie was being hustled out of the Lizard Ring by lizard-people, Justus by her side.

Soon the Great Salamander stood alone in the Lizard Ring, all other creatures having fled or lying wounded and dead.

Keiron pushed aside Badrur's smothering hand and cried out in anguish across the sand, "Cassie. Where are you? Cassie."

She heard his despairing cry and looked back. A cold sensation, like an icy finger, rang down her back, as if she was being cut in two.

In all their twelve years, the twins had never been separated. They had lived side by side, like the halves of one person. The anguish of their separation stabbed them to the heart, and as the desert space between them grew, the pain grew more acute.

CHAPTER 5

In the next few days Cassie endured the strangest journey she had ever experienced. She was strapped to the back of one cold lizard after another, changing creatures every hour or so. She kept her eyes shut for most of the time, for it was difficult to see anything but the scaly neck of the lizard from the position she was in. Her body moved with the rhythm of the lizard's swaying body, lulling her into a half-sleepy state. She was cool on her front, where she made direct contact with the lizard's skin, and too hot on her back where the sun beat.

In the hottest hours they all rested in the shade of dusty bushes or rocks, or burrowed into the sand, and they travelled in the cool of the night.

Cassie went from discomfort to stiffness to aches all over, and then beyond that into a state of numbness and exhaustion. Justus did his best to help her, bringing food and water, fanning her during the rests, speaking to her comfortingly; but the rest of the lizard-people treated her as little more than cargo, or so it seemed to her.

"Why don't they speak to me?" she asked Justus during one of their rests.

"They are worried about the Lizard Ring. They are frightened that Badrur and his monsters will return to it and dig it up and..." He swivelled his eyes around to see if he was being overheard. "You and your brother led Badrur to think he should search for the Shield there. They partly blame you."

"Oh," Cassie murmured, surprised and dismayed. "But that's not fair."

"I tried to warn you," Justus muttered.

"I'm sorry," said Cassie. "You should have told us why, though. I still don't know why the place is so important to you."

Justus slithered away from her. He would like to have told her, but the fewer people who knew the better.

At last they reached the underwater caverns where the lizard-people lived. Cassie was so stiff every movement hurt and she could hardly stand. She felt her skin was made entirely of itching sand.

She had to wriggle through a smooth hole in the rock. Hands pulled her in and she got shakily to her feet at the entrance to a dimly lit tunnel.

"This way," said Justus, and he led her through a maze of tunnels, often so low she had to shuffle along bent double, the floor always inclined steeply downwards.

They came out into a huge, breathtaking cavern. Reflected in a dark pool of mirror-like water, stalagmites and stalactites met to create fantastically coiled and glistening pillars and arches. Lizard-people lazed beside the water and sat on the many rocky ledges that rose in irregular steps; others were swimming lazily or sat half-submerged on rocks. For a moment Cassie forgot the ache in her body, the pain in her head – the cool shadowy majesty of the place, contrasting so starkly with the endless dust and space of the desert, overwhelmed her. A bluish light filtered down from hidden apertures in the roof, like the light through ancient stained-glass windows, and she was reminded of the mysterious serenity of the Chapel on North Island where the Golden Helmet had been found.

She yearned to be able to slide into that cool dark green water and wash the smothering dust from her skin; gesturing towards it, she asked Justus, "May I?"

The lizard-people nearby had risen to greet Justus. They were making a great fuss of him: the news that he had survived a scorpion sting had gone before him and now he was to them someone special, marked out to be a future leader.

But when they heard Cassie's request, there was a swift change of mood. They swivelled their heads and thumped their tails. "How dare she!" was the unmistakable message of their movements, and Cassie stepped back in confusion.

"I'm sorry," said Justus. "It's only for lizard-people."

The noise had attracted Tornius, the leader of the lizard-people. He approached them from around the pool, a group of Elders behind him. Justus felt nervous: how would the leader react to a chosen successor, and a mere boy at that?

"We are pleased to see you, Justus," Tornius said, nodding, although his eyes said something different.

"You must tell us all in detail how you came to survive the sting. Much depends on it, and the circumstances, as you know." The Elders nodded their agreement.

Tornius turned to Cassie. "Was it necessary to bring a human child in here?" His voice grew cold. "Is she not in league with the Queen?"

"The Queen is her enemy," Justus hastily explained. "And she was the one who drew out the sting. She saved my life, and now I am bound to look after her."

Tornius nodded thoughtfully, examining Cassie closely. "Then, Justus, while she is here, she will be your responsibility." Everyone knew what he meant by that, and they looked at Justus with some pity. "Take her away. We will talk to her later. And then return for the meeting, Justus. As a Chosen One, you will now be entitled to be present at the meeting of the Elders. We would hear what has been happening at the Ring."

"Follow me, Cassie," said Justus, and obediently she did so; she wondered whether she was a prisoner or a guest: it felt like somewhere between the two. They wound through more limestone tunnels, past many hollowed-out rooms where lizard-people slept or ate or lay curled up in serpentine heaps together. He led her into one such room. "This is mine," he said. "You can stay here."

The room was bare and dark.

"You must be thirsty and hungry. I will bring you something."

"Justus, why have I been brought here? Please tell me."

"Tornius wishes to find out all you know about the Queen. And why you came here. Who you are. The Shield." He shrugged apologetically.

"I wish you'd left me with Keiron." She was sorry the minute she said that. She saw the regret in Justus's green eyes.

"I'm sorry. I had no choice, it is our way. Tornius might question why you are here, but if I hadn't stuck by you, he would have questioned me far more fiercely. We live by strict and ancient rules."

"Yes, I can see that."

"You must be worried about Keiron."

Cassie sighed. "I miss him."

"Badrur won't hurt him, not when he's the key to finding the Shield."

"Yes, I suppose so," she murmured, cheered a little.

She looked about the dim and dank little cave. The prospect of spending time here did not please her. "Once I've been questioned," she said, "what then?"

"I don't know. Perhaps you will be sent back to the Palace. They say your father has been taken there. You'd like to be with him?"

She nodded thoughtfully; there was some comfort in that, despite the presence of the Queen. "But now, Justus, what I need, more than food or even drink, is water to bathe in. Don't tell me that's not going to be possible."

Justus grinned. "Come this way then, Cassie," he said. "I have a secret pool of my own."

He led her through further winding tunnels to a natural chute in the rock. She peered down it and could see water glinting below. "Watch," he said, and he slid down. There was a splash, and she could see him bobbing about in the water. "Come on," he shouted.

The water was so cool, she drew in a sharp breath of air as she splashed in, and then it closed over her head: for a few seconds the world was dark and muffled. She surfaced, gasping and laughing. Nothing – not anything in her life, she thought – had felt so delicious as that moment. With inexpressible relief, she washed herself of the grime that had stuck to her body during the long journey. Feeling free at last, she splashed about with Justus, raced him from side to side of the pool, floated on her back, and used him as a float to drift on. She never wanted it to end.

She emerged with her clothes and hair clean for the first time in days and the aches in her muscles, the soreness of her skin, half-eased away.

When they got back to his cave she sat on the rocky floor. "I will get you some dry leaves to lie on," Justus said apologetically.

He left her alone. The silence descended like a curtain. "Keiron," she murmured to herself in sudden anguish. "What are you doing now? What is happening to you? I know you're all right, I'd feel it if you weren't... *But I miss you so.*" She had been talking to him in her head ever since they had been torn apart; but now in the remote darkness of this cave, among creatures that were at best ambivalent towards her, she felt the gulf between them even more acutely. She dropped her head on to her knees and allowed herself to weep a little.

Justus returned with some other lizard-people, carrying great handfuls of dried leaves which they scattered about her. Cassie wiped her eyes and smiled her thanks.

"You have been crying," Justus said when they were alone again.

"My brother. I miss him. I'm afraid for him."

Justus nodded slowly, trying to understand her. "We are all brothers and sisters here," he said. "We do not know our parents."

Cassie looked into his large liquid eyes. "Is no one special to you?"

"In the first few weeks we do have one foster parent, but we don't remember who they are. Only Tornius and the elders are special to us."

"But why don't you have a family?"

"We all hatch from eggs," he explained. "No one knows who laid them or fertilized them."

"So you do not understand my feelings for Keiron?"

Justus blinked. "I feel the love you have for him."

"You do?"

"Yes, it is like the love that surrounds us all in these caverns. It binds us together."

"Then perhaps we do understand," said Cassie, after a pause. "And you will understand too, that he and I must be together. We always have been, up till now. Why don't your people rescue him from Badrur?"

"The odds are too high. His monsters, his scorpion-guards..." He shrugged.

As they talked, Cassie was visited by lizard-people curious to view at close quarters a human child from another island. Justus introduced each one, but to her they all looked much the same. Their faces were human, as were many of their gestures; she could distinguish little between them in the dim light. But she got a feeling that, because of the way she had saved Justus, they were better disposed to her than her reception had suggested. One even said, "Don't mind Tornius, child. He is always on his guard. And this is a bad time for us. He is on edge."

"Yes, I understand," she answered. "You all fear for the Lizard Ring very much, don't you?"

"We do," several said at once. "Our future lies buried there."

"How so?"

But they would not say.

Keiron had been thinking of his sister too. Twice he had escaped from the scorpion-guards and run wildly into the desert, calling out her name. He was at first almost overwhelmed by a sense of loss and anguish. It was as if someone had cut an invisible cord between them: his hands reached out into emptiness. He had never felt like this in his life before. Escape, shouting in the desert, screaming and hurling reckless insults at a half-amused Badrur – these were the only ways he knew how to relieve his feelings.

He calmed down gradually, out of despair and exhaustion. Will counselled patience, if only to get some peace himself. *She's not dead, and she's in safe hands*, he reminded Keiron time and again. *You'll soon be together again – and in the meantime, start exploring what it feels like to be just you.*

Just me? he answered grudgingly, in no mood to take reasonable advice.

Someone who exists on their own. Most of us have to do that soon after we're born.

That seemed like some kind of betrayal to Keiron and he snapped, *Why should I?* But he knew his manikin was right.

They turned to more immediate concerns.

Will said musingly, *Roots without trunks or leaves. It's puzzling. Why don't they grow?*

I'm not with you.

Down there in the sand. Something buried. Dormant. Like seeds waiting to sprout. Waiting a long time.

Doesn't that happen all over the desert? Seeds waiting patiently for rain?

Yes, but these aren't plants.

What else can they be?

Something to do with the lizard-people. Something they want to protect.

Bones, I should think. Of their ancestors.

But bones don't wait patiently for life.

Ghosts, then.

Will was silent. He couldn't quite get to the bottom of it.

"Whatever's down there," said Keiron, "the lizard-people want us to leave well alone. It must be something very precious to them."

Why on earth did he say that aloud? He blamed himself later for doing so, for Badrur, about to enter his tent, overheard it. Of course, Keiron protested that he meant nothing by it, and put forward his theory that this was an ancient burial ground, but the more he protested the more certain Badrur became that this was where they should search for the Shield.

"Why would the lizard-people bury it here?" he countered in desperation. "If it was here, they would find it and use it to bring rain, wouldn't they?"

"They would," said Badrur, "if they ever dug here. But this is the one place on this island where no one ever has dug, precisely because it is a sacred place."

Keiron stared into Badrur's snow-white face, into his cunning dark eyes, at his thin lips, at the sand glistening in his thick black mane of hair, knowing that the prince's logic was too strong for him to unwind. "There must be plenty of places in the desert where no one has looked," he said feebly.

"Of course. But the Shield was lost among ruins, or in ancient buildings, in cities. I do not believe it simply disappeared into the desert. Why should it? No, it is hidden in some place such as this. I feel it in my bones."

"Well, it is not here," Keiron said, feeling defeated. "I have asked."

"You will understand if I don't believe you," Badrur smiled ironically, getting up to go.

Soon after this, the first shattering blow against one of the rocks in the Lizard Ring splintered the air. Keiron pulled aside his tent flap and saw a dragon-like monster that brought back to him vivid and horrible memories. He was back in the Mansion on North Island with his father. This same creature had crashed through the upstairs window of their home and with awesome power was smashing everything in its path with an incredibly tough and indestructible snout. It reduced floorboards and chairs to splinters, it hacked its way through thick oak doors, it reduced his father's study to ruins... Now it was hammering at the rock with its snout. This was a tougher thing to shatter; it took many blows before cracks began to appear in the rock. The dragon-like creature, half as big as the rock itself, thudded incessantly, goaded on by Badrur.

All at once the rock, with its precious lizard etchings, suddenly seemed to explode, sending bits of rock shooting in the air. The dragon-like creature staggered back, dazed by the shuddering effort. Badrur scrabbled among the rocks, helped by the scorpion-guards, pulling the rubble aside in the hope that the Shield would be revealed.

Keiron watched them, his hands on his hips. "How can a shield be hidden inside a rock?" he asked when Badrur looked up, scowling and dusty.

Badrur slithered down the heap of rubble. "Did it never occur to you to ask how there came to be a ring of rocks in the desert? That's not a natural formation, is it? And where rocks can be placed in a ring, so can a shield be buried. One of these rocks might have a hidden cavity."

"I've already asked the rocks." He made the mistake of sounding scornful, and his tone was too much for Badrur. The prince lunged out and sent Keiron reeling into the sand. "Keep your wit to yourself, boy," he muttered.

For several more days the dragon-like creature attacked the rocks. It needed a couple of hours' rest between each one, and by the time it had finished, it had knocked itself so crazy that Badrur ordered it to be dragged out into the desert and left to die. He surveyed the rubble all around him, furious that Keiron had been proved right.

"Why don't we go back and search the ruined city," Keiron suggested, but the idea that the Shield was *here* had grown in Badrur's mind to such obstinate proportions, he answered with a curt order to the scorpion-guards and monsters, "Dig here in the circle. The Shield must be in the sand."

He mustn't, Will murmured, horrified.

But why not?

We shall soon see.

In the ruined city, the lizard-people who had survived the fierce little battle with the monsters slithered out of the dome. Alerted by a sixth sense, they moved at great speed across the desert towards the Lizard Ring. What they feared above everything was about to happen: they heard the mute cries of the unborn, no more than a pulse in their brains, but unmistakable. It filled them with profound anxiety – and anger.

The Great Salamander, gouging out huge shovels of sand with its giant claws, discovered the first ancient lizard egg. It lifted it out of the deep hole it had dug and rolled it along the sand towards Badrur. The egg was about the size of a man's head. He looked at it suspiciously, then held it out to the Great Salamander. "It's just a lizard egg," he said, disappointed. "You might find it to your taste, though. Break it open."

At that precise moment the small party of lizard-people slithered up behind the mounds of rubble. To their utter dismay, they saw the Great Salamander crack open the egg with a blow of its claw. Viscous liquid dribbled down. Curled in the broken shell was an inert baby lizard. The Giant Salamander tipped it into its mouth, and chewed with evident satisfaction. In the silence they could all hear the crunch of the baby lizard's bones.

Badrur and his monsters had discovered the lizard-people's most precious secret. Their future. And with one crunch of a dripping jaw, the monsters were setting out to destroy it. This struck at the heart of the lizard-people's existence, and they were incensed.

There were not enough lizard-people to mount a successful attack; but that didn't stop them. They streamed into the ring, shooting venom in wild, glistening arcs. There was a fierce and hideous fight that seemed to Keiron, cowering behind a pile of rubble, to go on for ever.

Then the lizard-people, overcome by the opposition, withdrew as quickly as they had come, leaving several wounded and dead behind.

Cassie slept a good deal at first; and Justus kept her company when he could.

She grieved quietly for Keiron's absence – it was like an ache in her heart. She thought of Tara the wolf-girl, too, whom she had befriended on North Island and who had become like a sister to her; but that only made her sadder, for Tara was dead, killed by the Child and buried in a forest; how she wished she had Tara's wolf-skin to comfort her now. And she thought of her father: had he arrived at the palace yet, and had he fully recovered from his fall?

She tried leaving Justus's cave, but her way was always blocked by silent, watchful lizards.

"You must come now," said Justus on the second morning of her stay, although it had seemed much longer. "Do not be afraid of Tornius. I have spoken to him about you." He led her into a cave so high its ceiling was lost in the shadows. Light filtered through holes and cracks and shimmered in water reflections on the walls. Lizard-people lounged everywhere, watching her intently.

On a rocky platform stood Tornius. He looked no different from the others except for an unmistakable air of authority about him. His eyes blinked slowly as she was brought in front of him.

"I am told that in your own country you are the ruler's daughter," he began. He could not quite keep the scepticism out of his voice.

"Yes," said Cassie. She was glad to be reminded of it and she lifted her chin a little higher. "Why are you keeping me here?"

"You led our enemies to the sacred ground. We have just heard that they have begun to smash the rocks on which our history is written. Soon they will be digging up our future."

"Your future? I do not understand."

Tornius glanced at the Elders questioningly; several nodded.

"A few generations ago," he said, his voice ringing out in the vast cave, "our ancestors lost a great battle with the scorpions and were driven into these caves. They feared for the future of our race, for we need the outdoor life to be fertile. And so, as a precaution, they laid eggs deep in the sands of the Lizard Ring. Those eggs are dormant. They will not hatch until the rains, that we all wait for, fall and penetrate deep enough to touch them. That was the wisdom of our Elders."

Cassie did not quite understand this but she had the sense to say, "I did not know. Justus would not tell us. I'm sorry."

"Here in these caves, our race is slowly dying. We lay fewer and fewer eggs." There was a mournful sound, halfway between a sigh and a hiss, from the lizard-people. "We need the sunshine and the bright air. We need freedom." There was a thumping of tails at that. "And the waters keep receding."

His eyes flared angrily. Cassie instinctively shrank back. "The eggs in the Lizard Ring are our future. And now a messenger comes to tell us that they are about to be devoured by monsters." The lizard-people hissed their anger and dismay.

Cassie suddenly understood it all. This ancient race, heirs to the island, driven into dark caves by the tyranny of the Queen and the scorpion-guards, slowly dying for want of light and freedom, had pinned all their hopes for survival on the eggs in the Lizard Ring, waiting quietly for the rains to hatch them. And now, she and her brother had attracted Badrur and his monsters to that very site. She blenched. No wonder they felt so ambivalent towards her.

Cassie glanced around and noticed the fear, the anxiety, the nervous dread in their eyes and in the flicker of their tails. "I'm sorry," she said with feeling. "I did not understand until now." She knew she sounded ineffectual, but she sensed her words had done some good.

But it was no wonder she had been kept practically a prisoner.

She moved on to the defensive. "My brother, my father and I hate the Queen and Badrur and the scorpion-guards and the monsters as much as you do. We don't like what they're doing."

"So Justus has informed us."

She glanced swiftly at her friend. "I saved his life, remember," she said quietly, giving him a little smile. "And I would save all of your lives if I could."

There was a rustle of movement among the listeners, a flicking of tongues and twitching of tails.

"And that is why you were not left to die with the monsters," one of the Elders interposed.

Cassie could not help flinching at that. She looked into Tornius's dark, green eyes for some signs of compassion.

"You see," he continued, "there are two ways of looking at your future, human-child. Either you die for making our enemies think the Shield is buried in the Lizard Ring, or you live for saving Justus and marking him out as a future leader. So far, you have been fortunate. He has pleaded well for you, and the Elders have been touched."

Cassie swallowed hard. She had not realized things had been so finely balanced.

Tornius turned and conferred with the Elders.

Justus squeezed Cassie's arm encouragingly and whispered, "Don't worry. You've made a good impression." She flashed him a grateful glance, aware of how much his pleading for her life had swayed the Elders.

Tornius turned to speak to her again."We have listened to Justus, who, as you saved him from the sting, was duty bound to plead for your life. We have considered your position too in relation to our enemies. And we have decided to trust you." He frowned at her sudden smile. "But only up to a point. We are not ready to release you yet. You may be useful to us. You may have the freedom of the caves, and we shall make your stay more comfortable, but you must not try to leave."

Cassie tried to put a brave face on it. She was safe, then, for the time being; but still separated from her brother and her father, still a virtual prisoner. Surrounded by all these glistening lizard-people with their large eyes and flicking tails, she felt very lonely. How much longer would she have to endure this?

But as soon as Tornius and the Elders had left, she was surrounded by lizard-people, who congratulated her, invited her to their caves, offered her titbits of food and shells of water, and made her feel that, having passed some crucial rite of passage, she was one of them. The lizard-boys and girls, in particular, stayed with her, plying her with questions about life on North Island, about Temple Island and the goddess Citatha, and inviting her to play their games.

Cassie was enjoying a game which involved hitting a ball with the tail and catching it in the mouth – she couldn't join in, but she kept the score – when Justus appeared. "Come with me," he said, somewhat conspiratorially. "I think you should see this."

He led her through winding passages to a place where there were several caves full of sandpits. In one of these, a few lizard-women sat around the edge of the sand, watching it intently. They seemed a little uneasy at Cassie's appearance, but Justus reassured them. Cassie settled down beside Justus, wondering what she was about to see.

"Look," said one, pointing at the sand. There was a movement under the surface. A tiny lizard wriggled a snout up out of the sand, then stuck its whole head out. It blinked and looked around. With a great effort, it pulled its little body out of the sand and sat there, panting.

"It is much too small," one of the lizard-women lamented, shaking her head.

Her voice attracted the hatchling. It wriggled over to her. Delighted, she curled her arms around it and licked it clean.

After a few minutes, Cassie whispered to Justus, "Are there any more?"

"There should be many more," he said anxiously. "It is past their time for hatching." But no more hatchlings appeared.

"Shall we dig?" one of the lizard-women asked Justus. He was momentarily surprised that they should be asking him, a mere lizard-boy, until he remembered his new status. He nodded. The lizard-women dug down to the eggs, scattering the sand in their haste. They lifted the eggs and put them to their ears, listening for signs of life. Cassie noticed how sad their faces grew.

"Break one open," Justus said.

They cracked open one of the eggs. Inside, curled in transparent slime, lay a lifeless little lizard, still half-formed, off-white in colour. Cassie took one look at it and averted her eyes. "How often does this happen?" she asked, dismayed.

"More and more frequently. Sometimes not one survives a whole batch."

"Not one?" she echoed helplessly. "I'm sorry, Justus."

"Now you understand how important the eggs in the Lizard Ring are," he said, as he led her away. "They won't be puny or dead like these."

That evening, Justus came to say goodbye. "We are leaving now," he said. "It has just been decided. Most of us are going to the Lizard Ring to see what we can do. Our future is being destroyed there. Make friends with those who stay behind and they will look after you."

"Take me with you."

He shook his head. "I have already asked that. Tornius was against it; he said you would slow them down. And besides, what could you do?" He turned to leave.

"But if they're wounded I could..."

But Justus, in a hurry to leave, did not hear her.

"Be careful," she cried after him. "And look after my brother."

She scrambled after him and watched him join the stream of lizard-people pouring out of the cave entrance. He turned briefly at the entrance and waved to her. There was a lump in her throat as she waved back.

Keiron was itching all over from insect bites, which made his nights terrible. How he missed his sister's healing fingers! And how he missed her! He too talked to her during the long, sweltering, dusty days and the shivering nights in his flimsy tent. He tried telepathy – he knew twins were supposed to be able to send thought messages to each other – but it didn't work. Ironic – he could talk in that way to inanimate things, but not to his sister.

Many times he had looked longingly at the stony desert, thinking if only. . . But Will was there to exercise caution. *You'd die out there*, he'd say, *and the vultures would feast on your flesh.*

Yes, thank you, Will. I get the message. But you can't blame me.

Just wait. I can't believe the lizard-people are going to let this desecration go on for much longer. Badrur is digging up their future and the monsters are devouring it.

A few nights later, he woke to the sounds of battle. The lizard-people, combining forces from the caverns and the ruins in a vast rippling green-and-gold wave, had sped silently up to the remains of the Lizard Ring. There they had launched a desperate and belated attack on the slumbering monsters and unsuspecting scorpion-guards.

Keiron and Will were caught in the middle of it, and no one there but Justus cared anything about them.

Chapter 6

While all this was happening to the north of the island, a darker, more destructive force had landed on the east coast: the Child. She looked like the offspring of a giant, chubby and defenceless; but she had no soul, and as such, she fed on death and destruction. She could kill at a touch; and each time she killed, she absorbed something of the energy of the dead, and grew a shade more in size. She was taller than a man.

She had a mysterious and invisible protective force around her, too, which repelled missiles. This is not to say that she was indestructible: she needed food and water like any living being, even though she could go for long periods without either.

She had been drifting on the currents of the sea for some time now, having set sail from North Island in pursuit of Prince Badrur. Once, not long after Cassie, with her gift for life, had brought her back from the dead, the Child had met him in the woods. As they gazed into each other's dark, fathomless eyes, a mysterious but inevitable bond had formed between them. Badrur feared and detested her, but she had dogged his footsteps ever since, as the one fixed point in her lonely life.

Drifting monotonously on the sea, she had grown hungry and thirsty; and in the growing heat of the sun, she had become dehydrated, sleepy and delirious.

Her broken ship was at last sucked into hot currents that swirled out from the undersea volcano just off East Island. There, she was pushed on a swell of steaming water towards the coast. Her ship crashed into rocks and became wedged at a drunken angle. She clambered off it thankfully, giving it a kick and splintering it for good measure. The seawater was almost scalding, and she splashed, crying and angry, to the shore.

There was no sign of any life. Just an undulating desert of grey volcanic ash and sand strewn with twisted rocks and tufts of stiff, struggling grass. Weak as she was, she set off across the landscape, a giant, thin, dazed, monstrous child, her feet burning, her eyes half blinded by the fierce light.

She soon learnt to travel in the cool of the night. Some instinct for survival took her in the direction of a small, scrubby oasis. There, desert travellers scattered in alarm and scorpion-guards tried without success to attack her.

She sat by the well, drinking bucket after bucket of the warm brown water; and slowly the dark light came back into her eyes. Travelling from deserted hut to tent, snatching up all the food she could find, she gorged herself after her long seaborne and desert fast.

The camels alone seemed unafraid of her. They watched her with lugubrious eyes and sceptical grimaces. They suffered her rough strokes with patience. The largest camel groaned under her heavy weight. She surveyed the wreck of the oasis with satisfaction.

She followed a trail lately made in the sand by a caravan of traders. Eventually she came to the craggy sandstone cliffs, eroded into fantastic shapes by the scouring wind, in which Badrur's cave dwellings had been carved long ago.

Here she was buzzed by more scorpion-guards. With quick, cunning lunges, she was able to snatch some of them from the air and squeeze the life out of them. Their stings made no more than a mildly irritating itch in her skin.

She climbed up the worn steps to the caves. In the biggest cave she found Prince Badrur's black cloak. Nothing but the presence of the prince himself could have made her happier. She swirled the cloak behind her and let it settle over her sunburnt nakedness. She snuggled into it.

She waited for several days and nights for his return, sleeping a good deal of the time, playing with and feeding the camels when she was awake.

She explored the cave dwellings. On the walls were crude drawings by previous desert dwellers, mainly of lizards, other animals and plants; she tried tracing over them with her stubby fingers, until she got bored with that. She wandered deeper into the connecting passages at the back of the caves.

And then she stumbled on a passage, just big enough for her to shuffle along with her head bowed; it sloped down and down into the rock and seemed to go on for ever. The floor was covered with sand, and she picked out here and there a human footprint which she assumed to be Prince Badrur's. It was dark here, and cooler. There were air vents in the ceiling, and from time to time she pressed her face to them to refresh herself and to remind herself that there was an outside world not far away. She went on and on, losing track of time, even of day and night. Sleep overcame her several times, curled up in Badrur's cloak, but in between she kept on through the seemingly endless tunnel, the prospect of meeting Badrur always before her. His footprints were her guiding light.

Eventually, the sandy rock began to change in colour and texture, and the tunnel gradually widened. She was able to stand upright and move quicker. The tunnel became a series of underground vaults.

She knew she had reached human habitation when she came across piles of lumber half obscured by dust and sand: old furniture, broken toys, rusting weapons, once magnificent robes now eaten away by insects. She was rummaging curiously through these, when she heard a door open at the end of the tunnel. A servant stood there, intending to dump a chair she had broken, in the hope that it would not be discovered. She saw the Child, froze, dropped the chair, shivered back into life, and fled with a panicky wail.

The Child was so used to inspiring fear and flight in those she encountered, she barely noticed it. She peered through the door into one of the palace's basement chambers. She climbed the steps into the palace itself, murmuring with anticipation. Badrur was bound to be here.

But the rooms and halls and corridors of the palace

were empty; there was no sign, even, of the fleeing servant. She wandered the cool rooms and corridors, puzzled and frustrated. There were indications of life everywhere – clothes, half-eaten food, unmade beds – but no one was there, not even the pesky scorpion-guards.

Everyone in the palace, the Queen, her servants and bodyguards, had gone down to the gates in the outer wall of the palace gardens to witness the arrival of Lord Tancred. It was known that he had lost consciousness after an accident, and rumour had it that he had lost his wits: they were curious to see how he behaved. Other rumours suggested that he was bringing back the Golden Shield, and although most people discounted that, in their hearts they hoped that it was true. They crowded on to the balcony and around the gates to watch him as he approached on his camel.

The Queen stood on the balcony, under a canopy of gently waving fans. "Welcome back, my lord," she cried, giving a regal wave.

Wearily, he gave her a curt bow of his head, and looked at the little crowd that had gathered. Sensing their hopes, he held up his hands and said, "I return empty-handed. You see? Forced to return! You must ask your Queen why I have been forced to give up the search for the Shield." He glared at her to make his point.

She scowled inwardly, but smiled and said, "You have had a serious accident, my lord. It is not wise to suffer the rigours of the desert after such a fall, however clever your daughter is at making you feel better."

During the desert journey, resentment had slowly built up inside Lord Tancred, and he let it show now. "Empty-handed! Just when we might have been getting somewhere! And my children abandoned to the desert! Is this how you treat your most honoured guests?"

"Come, my lord, you misunderstand us..."

They squabbled in this pseudo-polite and prickly way all through the gardens, the train of servants and guards listening with interest. The Queen, annoyed at his loud and tactless complaints – perhaps the fall had really affected his wits? – determined then that she would confine him to the Archives, where he could bury himself in old parchment and scrolls; he was already beginning to irritate her.

At the turning in the path that led to the main entrance, he stopped and said, with a determination she found absurd and comic, "At the first opportunity, I shall leave this place and return to my children. Have you no heart? They need their father, especially with your evil son on the loose." His face was so screwed up with hate and loathing, she laughed. No one had spoken to her like this for ages – apart from her wayward son, of course – and the laugh became a little hysterical.

She laughed so loudly, the Child paused to listen; but the sound was not sufficient to tempt her away from her new discovery. She had wandered into the gardens at the back of the palace and had found one of the giant fountains. The cool water cascading over her head felt delicious.

Challenged by two timorous and startled scorpion-guards, she had great fun in chasing them. They tried to sting her, but their stings just fell away. She touched them both, felt their lifeforce course up her fingers, and saw them collapse and die. Each time it happened, she grew another fraction.

Then she discovered the spring. The Sacred Spring. And it put all thoughts of finding Badrur temporarily out of her mind. Its pure, burbling glow drew her like a magnet. She plunged into the water and began to climb up the slope, stepping from rock to rock. How wonderful the water felt splashing all over her! She squealed with pleasure.

She swatted and squashed dozens of frantic and scared scorpion-guards who were guarding the water. They did not stand a chance against her. She felt strong again, full of life.

Soon she was high above the palace gardens. The water swirled around her thighs. She stretched her arms above her head and in a fit of pure joy, she cried out, a wild, primitive shout that reverberated over the palace and its great gardens.

The Queen froze in her tracks. Tancred looked up in shivering bewilderment. Servants gasped and pointed. Scorpion-guards scampered in confusion. They stared in horror: some kind of monstrous child was standing in the Sacred Waters! Polluting it with her body! Sacrilege!

The Queen was staggered. Not just by the size of the Child, but by the fact that this direct and blatant challenge to her authority had been allowed to happen, with everyone watching. "What in heaven's name is that?" she hissed at the captain of her scorpion-guards.

The captain gibbered something in sheer terror.

"How dare she!" the Queen screamed. "I don't care who or what she is, get her!"

Tancred had a mental flash of the battle on North Island between his own forces and Badrur's monsters: the battle had been abruptly brought to an end by none other than this strange and giant Child! But how had she reached East Island? What evil design had brought her here?

The Child continued to climb. She couldn't bear to leave the water now, not even to find out who those people were who were shouting and waving. Badrur wasn't among them, that she could see. The cool water bubbled around her legs and splashed on to her chest. Badrur's black cloak was heavy with water now but she still clung on to it.

Gradually the slope evened out until she was wading through a level stream of clear water. The air was thick with flying scorpion-guards, and she swatted them away from time to time.

Then she came to a rocky formation covered with straggling green plants. The water gushed from a cave. She waded into the cave. It was really a deep pool of turbulent greenish water, replenished by a gushing, roaring flow from a hole in the cave wall, and overflowing to create the stream that fed the palace. This was the outflow of the Sacred Spring, the only source of clear, fresh, *flowing* underground water left in the island. It had once been much mightier, but like all the water on this burning island, its source was slowly drying up.

* * *

The Child swam all day in the Sacred Spring; she splashed about in the shallows, and made mud sculptures on the bank. She killed so many scorpion-guards that they began to clog up the water, and that gave her the idea of building a dam with their bodies. She piled them one upon another until she'd created a wall of them. The diverted water created widening pools beyond the banks, which made her squeal with delight.

The fountains in the palace gardens below began to cough and splutter, a terrifying portent for those in the palace of what was to come.

The Queen's rage smouldered and flared. She could not understand why the scorpion-guards did not kill this outrageous challenge to her authority.

Night came, and the Child wanted to sleep.

But she couldn't because of the roar of the water in the cave. It disturbed her so much, in desperation she seized handfuls of scorpion shells and swam with them across the pool to where the spring gushed. She stuffed them into the hole. At first the spring spewed them out again, and for a while there was a kind of struggle of wills between the two, but the Child prevailed. By plugging the spring with bits of scorpion-guards, she succeeded in reducing its flow to a trickle and silencing it.

Down below, in the palace gardens, the Queen, Lord Tancred, servants and scorpion-guards stood at the foot of the Sacred Spring and watched in dismay as it dried up. The night air, always so full of the stream's murmur, grew silent. The fountains ran dry.

The Queen was ashen-faced. She had grown hoarse during the day shouting at her guards to kill the Child.

Now she looked on with despair. This was her life-blood drying up before her eyes. Her power depended directly on the continuing flow of this spring. Her dynasty was founded in it. Her eyes grew glassy, her body immobile. She sank into a fear so profound it appeared she had lost the will to move. She had to be carried back into the palace by two servants, lifting her discreetly by the elbows.

She had forgotten her decision to have Tancred confined to the Archives, and he was left to roam the palace gardens alone, looking vainly for a means of escape. He became aware of a change in the sounds of the night. When the spring had dried up, the cicadas had stopped their incessant scraping, and for a while the silence had been eerie. Now a new sound was swelling, of people beyond the palace walls. They had got wind of what was happening and had begun to gather outside the gates, afraid for themselves, but perhaps scenting rebellion too.

At the Sacred Spring, scorpion-guards tried to take advantage of the Child's slumbers to unblock the flow, but the minute the water began to gush again, the sound woke the Child. She was furious and lunged out at them.

She hollowed out a space for herself in the crushed bodies of the guards that were blocking the spring. There she settled down to sleep. No one would dare touch the spring now, or disturb her.

Some days previously, out in the northern desert, a scorpion-guard alighted amongst the mounds of sand and rubble that was once the Lizard Ring and reported to Prince Badrur the first sighting of the Child. When he heard the scorpion-guard describe the monstrous Child riding over the desert towards the Cave Dwellings, he shivered. He had hoped to the point of certainty that the Child had perished at sea. Now she was back like a disembodied shadow looming across his path. He knew what havoc the Child could cause. What if she reached the palace?

He went out beyond the camp and raged, shaking his fist at the implacable night sky. This Child was like a curse on his life, his ambitions. She had ruined his chances of ruling North Island. Was she going to do the same here? How could he destroy her?

After he had calmed a little, he debated what to do. Continue the search for the Shield? Or return to the palace to try and defend it against the Child, should she go there? He paced the night sands, debating with himself.

At one point he strode back into the camp, tore aside the flap of Keiron's tent and dragged the sleeping boy out. "Is the Shield here?" he shouted.

"No," said Keiron. "I've told you that before. Nothing tells me that it is. You're wasting your time."

"*Then where is it?*" Badrur hissed, the frustration in his dark eyes blazing. He seized the boy by the neck and shook him.

Keiron could see the prince was near breaking point, and he was terrified, but still he shook his head defiantly.

In a rage, Badrur rifled through the boy's hair, found Will and held the terrified little manikin in the air. "I could snap this little toy in two," he said.

"No," Keiron shouted, trying to leap up and snatch Will back.

Tell him what he wants to know, Will squealed.

"All I know," Keiron said between gritted teeth, his eyes fixed on Will, "is that it's somewhere in the sky."

"In the sky?" Badrur repeated in disbelief.

Keiron nodded defiantly.

"How can it be in the sky?"

"I don't know. But it's in disguise, too. That's what I was told in the palace gardens."

Badrur could see that he had shaken the truth out of the scared boy. He surveyed the shadowy holes and mounds of the dig, the empty shells, the slumbering monsters and watchful scorpion guards in the moonlight, and knew that his time had been wasted here. *Up in the sky...*

"Curse you!" he shouted. He threw the dazed manikin on the ground and lunged at Keiron, cuffing the boy around the head, kicking at his squirming body. "You could have told me that before."

"You wouldn't have believed me," Keiron shouted at him.

Badrur knew that he spoke the truth: if the boy had told him that before, he would have assumed it was a lie to sabotage the dig. He gave one last swipe at the boy, growled his frustration, and strode away.

Keiron picked up Will and spoke soothingly to him. Will gratefully climbed back into the boy's hair. *Your ear's red*, the manikin said.

So would yours be, Keiron said ruefully, rubbing his sore ear. In truth, he hurt all over.

Badrur stormed around the camp rousing every

creature. "We're leaving. Now!" he shouted again and again.

By dawn, the remains of the desecrated Lizard Ring were deserted. Eggshells were blown about in the wind, and a few tough spiders dared to emerge from the rubble; otherwise nothing moved.

That night the lizard-people, led by Tornius, swarmed around the Lizard Ring. They had travelled at break-neck speed from the Lizard Caverns in a desperate bid to save their species.

They were puzzled by Badrur's desertion. When they saw the extent of the damage, they became distraught, and they went from one hole to another, lamenting each in turn. They gathered the remains of the egg-shells together carefully, as if they were sacred relics, and buried them in one of the holes.

But what to do about the eggs that still remained buried? They debated that for some time. The sacred Lizard Ring had been violated, that was certain, and the rest of the unborn should be moved to another place. But wouldn't the movement disturb them, perhaps wake them prematurely? They counselled long. By dawn Tornius declared that, as a temporary measure, they should move the remaining eggs to the ruined city; it was a risk they would have to take. They would put them in the dome, fill it with sand and seal it off.

Justus had been part of these discussions, and was listened to with more than the usual respect – except by Tornius, who seemed impatient each time he spoke and several times questioned his opinion or cut him off, implying that a mere boy's ideas could not have great weight. The meaning of this was not lost on the lizard-boy.

He looked for signs of his friend Keiron, knowing how worried Cassie was about him. Studying the footprints in the sand, he deduced that the boy was probably still alive and had left with the evil prince.

But what had made them all leave when the job was half done? Had they got news of the Shield's whereabouts? That was a possibility; it was one which caused much speculation.

For the next few nights the lizard-people dug deep in the sands of the Lizard Ring. As the smooth and fragile eggs were brought to the surface, they glimmered large and white in the moonlight. They listened to each egg in turn, relieved to hear no sounds. When all the eggs were gathered, the lizard-people carefully picked them up in their jaws, so that the eggs rested on their tongues and pressed against the soft roofs of their mouths.

They set off with their precious cargoes, and made it to the ruined city without one egg being cracked.

In the Lizard Caverns news of the desecration of the Sacred Spring, and the blocking of its water by the monstrous Child, had had an electrifying effect on the remaining lizard-people. They understood at once that this was a direct and potent challenge to their enemy the Queen. This was no time to sit in the shadows, waiting. They began to stream out of the caves. A few set off to inform the main body of lizard-people who were at the Lizard Ring; the rest got ready to set off for the palace.

"Take me with you," Cassie pleaded, but at first they would not listen.

"I know who this Child is," she explained in desperation. "She comes from my home. I helped at her birth. *She knows me.*"

After some anxious and hurried whispering among the lizard-people, she was allowed to hitch a ride, as before, on their backs. They sped across the desert, past oases with barely a pause, towards the city. Cassie rejoiced in being outside again, and tried to ignore the dusty heat that rose from the sand in shimmering waves.

They arrived in the city with the sun at its hottest.

The crowd was still milling about the palace gate, talking excitedly, waiting to see how events would unfold.

Cassie was left to roam more or less on her own. She eavesdropped on snatches of conversation and learnt, with a little leap of her heart, of her father's arrival. She had a great longing to be with him again. As she listened and watched, insignificant and unnoticed in the shadows, she felt so lonely she could have cried.

She came at last to the closed gates of the palace gardens. With reckless boldness, she hammered on them as loudly as she could, crying out, "Let me in. I demand to see my father, Lord Tancred."

Some of the scorpion-guards, peering over the balcony above the gate, recognized her. As they unbolted the gate, she turned to some lizard-people who, belatedly, realized that she was deserting them. "Tell Justus I am sorry, I have to be with my father. But I'll do all I can for you, if it's in my power." She slipped inside just as they rushed forward to try and snatch her, and the gate clanged shut in their faces. She ran towards the palace. Scorpion-guards stood in its doorway, bristling, and she veered round the side of the building into the back gardens.

She came in sight of the great arch through which the Sacred Spring usually bubbled. The lack of water, the silence, was strange. Water weeds, stones and rocks were shrivelling in the hot afternoon sunlight, and little wisps of steam curled up from the drying spring bed.

Cassie saw a figure of a man slowly climbing the rocky slope. She stiffened; he seemed familiar. Was it...? The man paused and turned.

Yes, it was him! Her father!

What was he doing climbing up the spring towards the Child?

"Father," she shouted in relief. "It's me, Cassie. Come back!" But her shout was half-strangled by fears for his safety.

He seemed not to have heard her. Sobbing quietly to herself, she climbed after him.

She was aware of the danger she was putting herself in. But deeper than that, she was aware she was climbing towards the one being she feared more than any other. She prayed that she would get to her father first.

CHAPTER 7

Badrur, Keiron, the monsters and scorpion-guards arrived at the Cave Dwellings just after dawn, having made rapid progress from the Lizard Ring.

"We will rest until nightfall," Badrur said.

Keiron was left to find a cave for himself. He was just settling down to rest, his body weary from the endless rocking of the camel's back, his head aching from the incessant wind that had hummed in his ears all night, when Badrur came in. "Here," the prince said, handing him a bowl of dried fruit and meat. "Eat. You'll find water in the well back there."

Keiron, ravenous, seized the bowl and began to chew with relish.

Badrur smiled. "It's good to see you losing your dainty manners, boy. We'll make a man of you yet."

"What are we going to do?" Keiron asked. "I don't fancy meeting that giant kid again."

"Nor I," Badrur muttered. "But she has to be stopped – somehow."

He turned to leave, then paused in the cave entrance. "Two hours of sleep, boy. Then you start looking for the Shield here."

Keiron groaned. He was heartily sick of looking for the Shield, which for him meant little more than endlessly repeating the same question and never getting a positive reply.

Badrur laughed. "Remember, that's the only reason I spare your life."

Two hours later a scorpion-guard roused him from his sleep. Bad-tempered, thick-headed, sticky with the heat and plagued by bloodsucking insects, he was forced to begin the interminable search again. He did it with extreme reluctance: he knew with startling clarity that if he found the Shield, not only would it fall promptly into Badrur's hands, it would almost certainly precipitate his own death too. Of course, there was always the possibility that its magic might protect him in ways he could not foresee, but this was an uncertain prospect at the best.

The scorpion-guard who accompanied him was plainly bored too. It often stopped to twitter excitedly to another guard, letting Keiron wander on alone. The boy wondered how he could best make use of this slender opportunity for escape.

What do you think, Will?

Will uncurled himself from a pocket where he had been dozing, and said, *I get a picture of tunnels, like a network of roots, beneath us. And...* He closed his little green eyes and cocked his head to one side as if listening. *There might be one long tunnel like a great tap root. If so, that's the one you want.*

Hope quickened in Keiron. He kept a careful lookout for anything that might be the entrance to Will's tunnels.

They came across the food store. Despite the scorpion-guard's half-hearted protests, Keiron filled the large pockets of his loose and grubby gown with dried food, and he slung two leather bottles of water around his neck.

In the middle of the afternoon, they took a rest. Keiron pretended to fall asleep. The scorpion-guard slipped away to get some water. As soon as he was out of sight, Keiron ran to the entrance of a tunnel he and Will had noticed a little earlier – *That could be it*, Will had said – and plunged into it. It was a gamble of course, but if he was tracked down he could always say he had got lost.

He picked up a stone and used it to scrape marks on the wall: at least by this means he could find his way back if he had to. He noticed footprints in the sand: human footprints mingled with oversized prints of bare feet. It did not take him long to guess who had been here before him. So this was no ordinary tunnel: the Child herself had travelled down here.

That put a different complexion on things. A bit further on he paused, sat in the sand, and debated with himself the wisdom of going down this particular tunnel. If he met her – the giant Child – coming the other way, he'd have no chance, his life would be dependent on her infant whim. But it looked increasingly likely that this tunnel led somewhere, not just back into the caves.

Somehow, he had to get back to the palace and find Cassie and his father. That was the ever-present ache in his heart. He could take his chances with Badrur, or try this tunnel. Well, try the tunnel first, he thought, it could well lead to the city, and if it didn't, he could always retrace his steps.

He set up a brisk pace. The relative coolness was a relief and the freedom from the flies and insects made him feel quite cheerful. To be on his own again, away from the threatening, glowering, taunting presence of Badrur, that was the best of all.

His eyes soon got used to the darkness. The tunnel straightened out, the ground was smooth with sand, and soon, like the Child before him, his limbs fell into a kind of hypnotic rhythm that made him lose sense of time and distance. He daydreamed about his sister, re-ran conversations he'd had with her, thought of all the terrible adventures they'd had together on North Island and of the wonderful ship-ride in the golden tunnel...

Will, he said, *you remember you told me to become more independent?*

I remember everything, said Will.

Well, if independence means doing without Cassie, you can keep it.

Of course.

You agree?

If independence meant being without you, I would hate it too, I think.

Now he tells me!

A small pile of sand had trickled down from the rocky roof. Keiron used it as a makeshift bed. Sleep eventually overcame him.

At the Sacred Spring, the late sunlight shone on the dried-up bed of the stream. It flashed glimpses of light from the backs of the lizard-people stealthily creeping up through the undergrowth on the stream's bank, and from the hard shiny shells of the scorpion-guards still clustered in grim silence near the spring entrance.

Cassie followed her father up the dried brook. She tried to catch him up, but the way was steep and her body was sore and stiff from her journey across the desert to the city. He reached the top of the slope before her and splashed forward through the pools of shallow water there.

Cassie paused halfway up the slope. Her father was out of sight now. She was vaguely aware of eyes watching her and of faint rustlings in the undergrowth on the bank, and she felt acutely uneasy. She dared not call out to her father, for fear of rousing the Child, who, because she was quiet, was probably dozing. She began to climb again.

There was just a chance of reaching her father in time and drawing him away, for he had paused in his progress. He was examining the fantastic mud sculptures the Child had made earlier that day.

But as Cassie climbed, a scorpion-guard caught sight of a lizard-person arriving at the top of the slope. There was a fierce flurry between them, when venom and stings were exchanged; hideous cries rent the air. Other lizard-people appeared, and more scorpion-guards entered the fray; a fierce battle flared up between the two enemies.

The Child woke with a start. The noise of fighting was terrific. She waded out to investigate and saw the gleam of thrashing, writhing bodies of lizard-people and scorpion-guards on the banks either side of her. She clapped her hands in glee. What fun!

Then she saw Tancred backing away from the fighting, a look of sheer terror on his face. His presence stirred a deep, unpleasant memory in her slow brain: where had she seen him before? She advanced uncertainly towards him, casting her eyes about at the fierce little battles that were being fought not more than a few feet from her.

Scared by the noise of the fighting and the looming Child, Tancred backed to the top of the slope. He kept his eyes warily on the Child and did not look where he was going. His feet slipped on wet weeds, his hands waved wildly in the air, and he toppled down; he half slithered, half rolled, down over the smooth stones towards Cassie. Then he hit his head and came to a halt.

Cassie bounded frantically up to him. "Father!" she cried, shaking him, but he did not answer. His head lolled, and his eyes stared blankly. She began to feel over his body for broken bones and torn muscles, that she might heal them with her miraculous touch; but then a darkness made her look up.

Like a great shadow, the Child, on top of the slope, peered down at her. It was an eerie moment. There was a flicker of recognition in the Child's eyes.

Cassie stood up, shaking all over. What should she do?

Suddenly she was surrounded by flying scorpion-guards, whirring angrily about her head. She crouched over her father to protect him, but they pushed her away. They lifted him bodily, gripping his clothes with their pincers, and carried him down to the palace.

The fear that he might be dead outweighed even the fear of the Child looming above her.

She was shivering all over, unable to move.

At the foot of the dried spring stood the Queen. Cassie understood at once that she owed her father's rescue to her.

Water from the partially unblocked spring began to trickle around her feet. Its unexpected touch made her scream.

"Come down, Cassie. Quickly," the Queen shouted. Cassie knew that she had little choice; besides, she had to be with her father, dead or alive.

By the time Keiron and Will reached the palace, they had lost track of time and distance, and Keiron had exhausted his precious supplies of food and water. He half-noticed in the gloom that the shape and texture of the tunnel walls had changed; but it wasn't until he stumbled on some of the lumber in the palace's underground vaults that he understood where he was.

We've made it, Will, he said excitedly. *This tunnel leads to the palace.*

Cassie's here, I think, said Will.

That set his heart beating fast. He stopped, closed his eyes, pictured her, and felt her distress. "Yes, she's here," he breathed excitedly, and the thought that he might see her again made him hasten forward.

A few minutes later they came up against the stout wooden door. To Keiron's dismay, it was locked. He looked into the keyhole: there was no key the other side. A pang of pure frustration made him groan aloud.

Don't say another word, said Will. He ran down Keiron's arm and wriggled into the keyhole. He stuck his head out. *I'll bring Cassie back to you, if I can.*

With his back to the door, Keiron slid down to the ground and rested his chin on his knees. He was thankful for the rest. He remembered another time, long ago, when Will had wriggled into the lock of the Chapel on North Island and opened the door for them. There, his father was lying on the altar stone, seemingly dead... He closed his eyes, and the story of that time flashed through his mind in vivid fragments, keeping him from worrying too much about his lonely predicament.

Will had seldom been separated from Keiron and he did not like it one bit. He was aware of how small and defenceless he was. He contemplated the flight of stairs to the ground floor of the palace: it seemed like a mountain to him. He leapt from one stair to another, pausing to steady himself after each leap, and he eventually made it to the top. He came to a junction in the corridor above the stairs. A servant appeared, trailing a long rug. He fell to the ground and curled his limbs, looking for all the world like a twig, but as the rug swept past him he got tangled in its long fringe and was pulled along with it.

They entered a bedroom. The servant bowed and said, "The extra rug you ordered, your majesty."

Will looked up in surprise. He was no more than a few feet from the Queen's golden sequinned gown.

"Throw it over him," said the Queen. "He's shivering."

As the rug was lifted, Will fell off. He scurried under

the bed. He watched the feet of the servant shuffle backwards and leave the room, leaving only the Queen's golden shoes: he noticed they were made of overlapping sequins like the scales of a fish, with a flame-like motif snaking up her ankles.

"Well, my lord," he heard her say, as if to herself. "You're not much use to me like this. And as for your hysterical daughter..." Will imagined her shrugging in disgust. "What shall I do with you both, eh?"

She was interrupted by a scorpion-guard. "Your majesty," said the guard. "The monstrous Child is blocking the Spring again."

The Queen spat and raged at the poor guard. Will cowered under the onslaught – what an incredible range of curses and insults and threats she had at her command! "Send for my son immediately," she shrieked at the terrified guard. "Perhaps he can lure this Child away."

When the sound of the Queen's feet and voice had died away at last, Will cautiously poked his head out and listened: he heard only Lord Tancred's steady breathing. He shinned up the rug and ran up the patient's chest. He tried slapping Tancred's cheek, pulling his hair, tweaking his ears, pinching his nose, but to no effect.

Then he remembered his mission. The Queen had mentioned Cassie. Where was she? He flitted from room to room, dashing across corridors, often just missing been seen by nervous servants and scurrying guards, always aware of the Queen ranting and raving not far away. He peered into the throne room: all was silent there. Then, at the foot of the stairs, he heard faint sobbing and he knew that he had found her.

He tugged at her long, grubby gown. She cried out in alarm; and then she snatched him up in delight. "Will, oh, Will," she cried, realizing at once that where Will was Keiron could not be far behind.

He wished he could speak to her, but his telepathy did not work with her, nor with anyone but Keiron. Never had he regretted that more than at this time. He had often thought that if he could speak to her in the way he spoke to her brother, she would have taken him more seriously and perhaps cared for him more. It did not seem fair, either: after all, she had woken the life in him, turned him from a bit of carved wood into a living being; she had as much right... But now he had to resort to gestures.

She looked at him with different eyes, too, as if he was a part of her brother, and she vowed to herself that she would not let petty jealousies and misplaced disdain for the manikin spoil the feelings she had for him. What bright green, courageous eyes he had!

As he gestured, she tried to understand what he was saying; and then she followed him cautiously back through the shadowy passageways. She heard the Queen raving, and she shivered at the violence of the language.

"My father," she murmured as she recognized the corridor down which he had been taken when they had been forcibly separated earlier by the Queen; but Will tugged at the strap of her sandal as if to say, *There is something more urgent you have to do.*

He led her to the basement door, and knocked on it.

"Keiron? Are you there?" she said, hardly daring to believe he was.

He was dozing, tired after his long underground trek, and for a while his whispered name seemed part of his dreams. Then he felt Will land in his hair and shout in his head, *Wake up, Keiron. Cassie's here.*

Those last two words were like a little electric shock. *Here?*

Other side of the door.

"Cassie, is that really you?"

"Keiron!" She was so relieved to hear his voice, to feel his presence, even through a stout locked door, she could not for a moment find anything else to say.

They peered at each other through the keyhole.

"Can you find the key?" Keiron asked.

She explained her position.

"Don't leave me again, now that we found each other," Keiron said. *Will. . .*

Yes, all right, you don't need to say it, Will sighed.

He scampered off again, this time in search of a key. Why, he wondered, was his fate to be so bound up with ancient keys and locks?

The twins sat with their backs to the door either side. They did not need to say how uncomfortable, even painful, their separation had been, nor of the relief they felt to be back together again. Cassie just said, "It's been horrible, Keiron," and he replied, "Never again."

Will peered into the Queen's own bedchamber. He had looked everywhere but here. This was going to take courage.

Water had been carried laboriously up from the basement pool to her chambers, and she was bathing in a vast bath, or rather lying in one muttering to herself, her eyes closed, her claw-like hands clasping the bath's edge. Petals clogged up the water and were scattered around the bath.

Will climbed up on to the bed. There lay a bunch of keys – there weren't many keys, for the palace had few doors to lock – and one of them was big and brown with ancient rust; he felt sure that was the one. Her back was to him, but he could not just tip the keys over the bed, the noise would give him away. He found a waist-cord among her clothes and used it to lower the keys to the ground. There was a little chink-chink when they touched the carpet, which made her open her eyes and listen. Then she rose from her bath – how scrawny she looks, he thought, like a gnarled old tree – and smothered her head in a huge towel. He took the opportunity and dragged the keys across the carpet to the corridor outside.

The rusty key fitted the lock.

The twins hugged one another. It felt wonderful to be together again; a new confidence surged through them.

"Run your hands over my skin, Cass," Keiron pleaded. "I'm a mass of old bites and sores and my muscles ache all over."

They found their father unattended. He was still unconscious.

Cassie ran her hand over him: nothing was broken. She turned her attention to his head. There was a fresh gash. She placed her hand over it and felt the crack in his skull heal and watched the skin knit together. Then she put her hand on his brow and kept it there, feeling his brain cooling. He woke with a cry and groans so loud they had to smother his mouth for fear that he would attract attention.

He sat up, rubbed his eyes, and as his sight focused, he smiled at them. A sane, warm, lucid smile. He held out his arms and murmured their names; they buried themselves in his hug, Cassie with tears on her cheeks, Keiron laughing in relief. They were together again, and for a while that was all that mattered.

CHAPTER 8

In the dome of the ruined city, the lizard-people finished covering with sand the eggs which they had so carefully transported across the sands, and which contained their hopes for the future. They sealed up all entrances to the building and posted guards all around it. They were uneasy: the wreck of the Lizard Ring and the destruction of half of the Dormant Ones (as they called the eggs) had profoundly shaken them.

They knew that the dome was a only temporary resting place for the eggs. Much discussion among the elders, much looking for signs and portents, much poring over maps and obscure cave drawings, would be needed in the weeks ahead before the site of another Ring could be found. Until then, their race was in peril.

When they returned to the Lizard Caverns they were surprised to find them all but deserted. As soon as they heard news of the Child and the blocking of the Sacred Spring, they became excited. This might be their chance. The city populace would be anxious about the sudden scarcity of water and the hike in its price; the scorpion-guards and the Queen would be distracted;

and Badrur and his monsters were probably out of the way at the Cave Dwellings. If they could get to the Palace of the Fountains in time, they might be able to invade it and topple the Queen.

Justus was as excited about this as all the rest. The last few days had not been that easy for him. He was in a curious position: the people kept a respectful distance from him now, knowing that he was marked out to be their leader one day; but the Elders still treated him like a child, pretending to consult him but often ignoring what he had to say. He suspected Tornius felt uncomfortable in having someone else ready to take over. He was often lonely, a position and a feeling he had never experienced before and which troubled him.

But he had something else on his mind: where was Cassie? He was conscious of his obligation towards her – she who had saved his life – and was aware too that he had left her exposed and vulnerable; once in the city, he would have to find her. In his newfound loneliness, he valued the friendship of the human children.

As he was about to set out with the others, his way was barred by Tornius. To his amazement, Tornius said, "You cannot go with us, Justus. Because you survived the sting, you know you will be my successor. It is possible that in the battle ahead I shall be wounded or killed. You must be kept here in safety."

Justus pleaded with Tornius; he explained about Cassie; but his leader was adamant. Indeed, Justus got the impression that Tornius almost got satisfaction in refusing him. The Elders nodded sagely, too, and he felt they were all against him in this. "You're still a boy, remember," Tornius said, patting him coldly on the shoulder, a slight curl of contempt on his lips. "There'll be plenty of time for you to prove yourself before I'm past it." The Elders laughed knowingly, and Justus was left feeling foolish.

In dismay, he watched them stream out of the caves.

Left almost alone in the caves, he brooded on his disappointment and sudden isolation. He didn't for a moment regret surviving the sting, but it had certainly made his life more difficult. He wondered about Tornius's motives. His leader, never very friendly to the young, had grown cold and correct towards him. He had even heard that Tornius had cast doubt on the sign, saying that he had not survived the sting on his own but by the sorcery of the human girl. Perhaps Tornius had his own favourites among the younger lizard-people; perhaps he was secretly grooming someone else for leadership. Was this his attempt to freeze him out and make him appear weak in times of battle?

When nightfall came, he had made up his mind. A future leader would not skulk in the safety of the caves while his people were out, possibly fighting for their survival. In fact, maybe this was a subtle test, or even a trap, set by Tornius to see how he would behave in such a situation: with caution or with courage? He stole out, determined to join his people and to find Cassie, regardless of Tornius's decree.

As the main body of the lizard-people set out for the

Palace of the Fountains, a scorpion-guard was alighting outside Badrur's Cave Dwellings with the Queen's orders that her son make his way at once to the Sacred Spring.

Badrur shuddered when he heard who was there, and what she was doing. As the scorpion-guard described the devastating effects the Child was having on the flow of water, effects which were rippling out into the city in waves of unrest, Badrur knew he had no choice: to turn his back on his mother at this point would put his own dynasty in peril.

He was already in a foul mood. He was annoyed that the boy had given him the slip. What chance had he of finding the Shield without him? Would the boy die lost in the labyrinthine tunnels of the cliffs, perhaps with the secret of its whereabouts? In a fury, Badrur had lashed out at the scorpion-guards and cursed them, but it had done little to assuage his frustration.

And now this!

Fuming, he mounted his Great Salamander and set off across the stony desert towards the palace, resenting every step he was forced to take. He left the rest of his monsters behind, their progress being too slow for the speed he needed.

At the Sacred Spring, the Child was sitting in her castle of mud. A tiny trickle of water still came from the spring, enough to slake her thirst and give her water to make the mud. She was pulling apart a scorpion-guard that had foolishly tried to attack her from above. Pulling away the hard outer shell of its curled body, she tasted the soft yellowish flesh. It was sweet and chewy. Delicious!

Here, she had everything. Food, water, mud, a cave to sleep in... She had never felt so happy.

She finished her meal and slung the scorpion-guard's shell and claws on to a growing heap of debris in the cave. Leaning against the mud walls of her castle, she was soon snoring, the steam rising from the mud all around her.

The Queen was sitting on her throne, her dark, wide eyes glittering intensely as she watched Lord Tancred pace up and down in front of her and listened to his seditious words.

The twins sat on chairs to one side, aware of the vast empty hall, of the dust swirling in the beams of sunlight, of the scorpion-guards crouching in the shadows. They too listened to their father's words. They marvelled at his quick recovery. He seemed to have lost his deference towards the Queen, and they could see that this both angered and confused her.

"You cannot lay blame for the Child at my daughter's feet," he was protesting.

"She brought her into this dismal life," the Queen retorted. "She meddled with nature. You told me that yourself. She is responsible for her, and thus for the incredible damage she is doing."

Cassie looked down at her clenched hands and swallowed hard.

The Queen glared at her. "She should lure the Child away."

"I don't think it would work," Tancred said.

"But you have to try it," the Queen cried. "It will be a while before my son gets here. The damage must be stopped now!"

"And if I refuse?" Tancred said softly.

"I will have you stung to death," she said, her eyes glittering. "I would deeply regret that, of course."

"Of course," Tancred said, aware of his children's alarm, determined to stay calm. "But what then?"

She looked up. "Then?"

"When – if – Cassie can draw the Child off? Or Badrur succeeds where we fail – for we are likely to fail in this, whatever your threats."

She shrugged. "You will be allowed to leave. Your son – " and here she looked daggers at Keiron – "has failed to help me find the Shield. I do not believe any more that he is capable of doing so."

"But we *have* to find the Shield," Keiron butted in.

"He's right," said Tancred. "We can't leave without it."

"Oh, you will leave without it, whether you find it or not."

A silence descended on the little group. The twins glanced at each other in dismay.

Tactfully, Tancred did not challenge this. He changed tack and began to plead for the rights of the lizard-people, and became eloquent in their defence; but this was hardly the best time to launch into such a prickly subject and the Queen soon lost patience with him altogether.

"Power lies in water here, not history," she said, rising from her throne dismissively, her eyes narrow and gleaming with impatience. "If you've nothing better to say..."

She swung round to look at Cassie. "Now, girl, it is time for you to climb up to that monstrous Child of yours and make her see sense."

Cassie went very pale.

Tancred stepped between them. "I cannot allow it," he protested, barely keeping his anger in check.

At a sign from the Queen, the scorpion-guards rustled forward and surrounded them with a ring of claws, waving antennae and beady eyes.

"I don't think you have any choice," she said.

Cassie rose. "I won't," she wailed. "I won't go near the Child. I can't.

"Oh, yes you can," the Queen hissed at her, "and you will."

Cassie felt her stomach churn so much, she leaned against the arm of her chair to steady herself.

"She's going to be sick!" Keiron exclaimed.

Cassie retched.

For the next two days they managed to hold out against the Queen's command. The tension gave Cassie fierce pains in her head, dark shadows under her eyes, a loathing for food. The Queen herself could see she wasn't faking it, and for a while, against her better judgement, she held back, knowing their resistance would soon crumble.

But as the unrest in the city grew, and as her scorpion-guards' loyalty began to strain under the pressure to protect the palace and harry the Child, she eventually lost patience. She came into Cassie's room, a look of such cold determination on her face the twins shrank back.

"Out! Now!" she screamed at Cassie. "Get that Child out of my Spring."

Keiron jumped up, swerved round her and ran into the passage. "Father! Father!" he shouted.

"Your father cannot come now," she called to him. "I've confined him to the Archives." She turned to Cassie. "I've waited long enough. Move!"

Two scorpion-guards shuffled up the passage towards them. Cassie saw she had no choice. With her heart beating hard and her head throbbing, she followed the Queen out of the palace to the foot of the dried-up spring.

"I'm going up with her," Keiron said defiantly.

Slowly they began the ascent. A couple of flying scorpion-guards hovered overhead, and others watched from the bank.

"What shall I say to the Child?" Cassie said, her eyes full of anxiety, her hands as she grasped the rocks weak with nervousness. "How can I make her understand me?"

Keiron shrugged.

In desperation, she said, "Has Will any ideas?"

But Will remained silent.

The sight of the huge, irregular circle of mud in front of the cave entrance made them pause. Strewn everywhere were bits of scorpion-guards, mainly shells and claws.

They could hear the Child splashing about in the cave pool.

"Are you ready?" Keiron asked, and he took his sister's trembling hand. She nodded. "Then let's call her."

They shouted, "Child, Child, come out. We want to talk to you."

The Child appeared around the side of the mud castle, brown and naked, her big feet splashing in the shallows. She stopped and looked at them quizzically.

She fixed her black eyes on Cassie. The faintest recollection came to her, of saying farewell to this girl in a forest; and then at that big noisy battle. She sensed the connection between them, and this made her feel strange – a confusion of tenderness, longing and hurt. She waded forward slowly, making strange noises, half laugh, half murmur, holding out her hands to Cassie.

"She's coming! Step back!" Keiron said.

But Cassie was too petrified to move.

With a few strides, the Child was looming over them.

Cassie looked into her dark and imploring eyes. She remembered doing that when the Child had been a baby and seeing, not reflections, not the soul, but a vast, deep expanse of space. Now at least, there was a hint of something human there, a gleam of longing, a note of puzzlement.

She closed her eyes, knowing that this was a supreme test. *Help me*, she cried in the terrifying emptiness. And then, as if at her bidding, there stepped out of the orange flicker of light behind her eyelids a cool, sleek, silver cat, so real that she could almost reach out and touch it. "Lead her to the water in the cave," the cat said, and it turned as if to say, *follow me*.

Cassie opened her eyes. Only a few seconds had passed, but now she felt different. "Follow me," she said, beckoning to the Child, and she waded around the other side of the mud castle, where the silver cat had disappeared.

Keiron stood, uncertain what to do. "Cassie," he cried.

"Stay there, Keiron," he heard her say. He watched the Child splash after his sister. He stood irresolute, wondering at the sudden change in his sister. *What shall I do, Will?*

As she says. She wants to be alone with the Child.

Cassie led the Child into the cave. She pointed and said, "Unblock the Spring." She said it several times, not knowing how much the Child understood.

The Child looked at her and the Spring and back again, several times. Then she reached out to touch the girl. Cassie swivelled away and pointed again at the Spring. "Unblock it!" she shouted, suddenly realizing that the strange courage the silver cat had given her might evaporate at any moment.

The Child recognized the note of command and splashed to the Spring outflow. She pulled away the rotting carcasses, the shells and claws, the mud and stones she had filled it with. Suddenly, the water burst through, washing the rest of the detritus away, and there was a great gushing turbulence in the cave. The Child danced in it, shrieking in delight.

Cassie watched her, fascinated. What a strange mixture the Child was: at this moment, more like a three year old than anything else; at other times, a blindly destructive force; and then, there was the eternity signalled in those black eyes, as if she was from another world.

Suddenly, Cassie's courage drained away. She had to get out. In a panic, she stumbled out of the cave.

Already the water was up to her thighs. She looked around for Keiron. He had been there a moment ago.

And then her heart was in her mouth.

Under the onslaught of the water, the huge mud castle was disintegrating before her eyes. It was collapsing in on itself and shifting in a mass. The pressure of the water was pushing it forward.

"Keiron!" she screamed.

He was crossing the stream behind the mud castle. As soon as it began to shift, he saw the danger. He scrabbled frantically to get out of its path, but he did not have enough time. The mud slide was upon him. He was enveloped in a great oozing brown sludge that pushed him towards the edge of the spring.

Down he went. Mud smothered him, rocks grazed and cut him, water buffeted him; his body was tossed from side to side. Dimly, in the terrifying flight, he was aware of Will clinging on to his hair, calling to him, and then he sensed that the little wooden manikin had been torn away. He reached the bottom of the spring, stunned, a leg and two ribs broken, a huge gash seeping blood down his forehead.

The mudslide flowed over him. He struggled to rise above it, but the mud was like a spreading shroud.

Cassie struggled through the fast flowing muddy water to the top of the spring. She could just see her brother struggling in the mud far below. She was beside herself with fear. Then she saw something green flash across the grass from some bushes. It slithered at great speed up to where Keiron was floundering.

She could not stay in that position any longer. The force of the water was tugging at her thighs, and she was in danger of being washed away herself. She waded towards the bank.

She had been aware that the Child had been splashing noisily in the water, half-lamenting the destruction of the mud castle; now, strangely, the Child was still and silent.

Cassie stopped and swivelled round; her heart missed a beat.

There on the opposite bank was Badrur, astride his monster. At the end of his lonely trek across the desert, he had come straight to the Spring.

With a sigh of impatience and fear, he turned his mount and lured the giant infant away from the Sacred Spring. His idea was to lead her into the desert far enough for her to get lost and die of dehydration. She ran after him on her stubby legs, laughing with delight.

Cassie watched them depart. Keiron! She must get to him. She waded to the bank, clambered up it, and then scrambled down the slope with all the speed she could manage.

There was no sign of him. Just mounds of shifting mud and angry flowing water. As she stood halfway down in a panic of indecision, the Queen and her father came hurrying over the lawn.

"He's all right," Lord Tancred shouted to her. "The lizard-boy saved him. But he's in great pain. Come down, Cassie, quickly."

Another great wave of relief. She was shaking all over now; but at least Keiron was safe.

As soon as she reached the foot of the now freely

flowing spring, the Queen said, "What about that monstrous Child?"

"I did what you wanted," she said, impatiently, her thoughts only for her brother.

"Then where is she?"

"Badrur turned up. He's leading her away somewhere."

"Ah," she smiled. She turned abruptly and left them.

In the palace, Keiron was moaning deliriously. Justus was trying to make him drink.

Cassie rushed up to the lizard-boy and hugged him. "Thank you," she cried.

Justus's eyes glittered. "I arrived just in time. I saw him tumbling down."

"But are you safe here?" she asked.

"The scorpion-guards won't attack me because I survived their sting," he reminded her.

As she healed her brother's broken bones and skin, Justus marvelled at the strange, intense expressions that flickered over her face. The lizard-boy recalled the way she had drawn out the excruciating pain of the scorpion-sting from his own body with the penetrating coolness of her hands.

Keiron opened his eyes and sat up. He looked at his damp clothes and gingerly felt his body. "Thanks, Cass," he murmured, knowing how inadequate that sounded. Seeing Justus, he recalled the mud slide, the shroud of suffocating darkness, the sense of sinking into a dark pit, and then of Justus's powerful claws pulling him out of it, into gasping, blinding sunlight. He threw his arms about the lizard-boy's neck and hugged him. Justus shrank back a little, not used to such displays of emotion; but he suddenly felt bound closely to these two human children, more than he had ever done before, as if they were three of a kind.

Keiron felt in his hair and patted his clothes anxiously. "Have you seen Will?" Their blank faces were enough. "He got separated from me in the water. He must be out there somewhere." His pleasure at being alive drained away and a look of despair passed across his face. "Come on, we've got to find him."

Keiron and Justus rushed out immediately.

Cassie paused at her father's side.

"Was it so bad?" he murmured, putting his arm around her shoulder.

"Seeing Keiron fall was worse," she said.

"Good," he nodded. "That's how it should be."

"You know," she said. "For a while, up there, with the Child, I did not think she was all evil. I mean, I know she killed Tara..." A little lump came into her throat as she said that. "And she seems to feed off death, but..."

"But?" her father echoed sceptically.

"Somewhere inside her, I think she's just like a little girl."

"Well, perhaps. But appearances are usually deceptive. Don't be taken in by that. Let's hope Badrur succeeds."

"Succeeds?"

"In getting rid of her somehow. Or we shall always be plagued by her."

Cassie nodded. "And if we are," she said, "I wonder

how big she will grow." Her father felt her shoulders shake in sudden fear and disgust.

"I must go and help look for Will," she said, disengaging herself. "Keiron will be devasted if he's lost. What will you do, Father?"

"I will try and talk to the Queen again. Try and make her see sense."

"She won't now, will she? Not now she's got the water back."

"Perhaps not," he sighed. "But it will put her in a better mood. I still have to persuade her to let us stay and continue the search for the Shield. She may have lost faith in that, but I haven't."

Will had struggled out of the mud and had been swept down the spring and into one of the underground pipes. Then he was pushed up another dark pipe by the pressure of the water.

Suddenly, he burst into daylight at the top of the main fountain! But he couldn't escape – the bottom half of his body was trapped. Try as he might, he could not wrench himself free, because the water had swollen his wood. He wriggled and heaved and strained to get out but it was no good. He was stuck.

Later, he could see Justus and Keiron scrabbling about in the spring and hunting along the bank. Some scorpion-guards were fussing around them. He saw Cassie racing across the garden to join them. How he wished he could call out to them. For the rest of the day he watched them hunting. Frustration alone could have killed him, he thought. As evening fell, he saw them trail across the garden, wet and forlorn. Crying out again, they did not hear him.

He saw Justus peel away from the twins and disappear into the undergrowth.

And then he was alone among the stars.

The twins took a long time to get to sleep that night; and they rose late the following morning. Cassie felt better than she had for a long time: she was reunited with her brother; her father was his old self again; and the Child had been drawn away from the palace by their enemy, Badrur. A brief respite, then.

If only they could find the Shield. Then they could quit this dreadful place for good.

Keiron missed Will's comforting presence and bantering advice and he was full of anxiety about him. He too was sick and tired of this hot, dusty, sticky island with its strange creatures, its cowed populace, its cold-hearted Queen and brutal guards: what a place! The only good thing they had met here, he decided, was Justus: a friendship had sprung up between the two boys that delighted him. But even that was laced with disappointment, for he knew that as soon as they had to leave the island – and let it be soon, he sighed – he would also have to leave this new friend behind.

And the hunt for the Shield! The burden of it had fallen on his shoulders, because of his "gift". What an ambiguous gift that had turned out to be! Would the Shield be worth all this grief? He seriously doubted it. What would happen if they simply gave up the search for it?

He voiced this question at a late breakfast.

"I don't know," said his father. "But it is not to be contemplated."

Keiron shrugged questioningly.

The Queen fixed him with her dark eyes. "What you're saying, boy," she said, "is that you've already given up the search for it, in your heart. Am I right?"

Keiron cast his eyes down and examined the rind of the watermelon he had been eating.

The Queen rose impatiently from the table. "Well, after what your father has said, I'm prepared to give you three more days," she said.

"Only three days?" Tancred echoed, alarmed.

"I have lost faith in your son's ability to find it," she said simply. "So what else do you have to offer? I'm sorry. Your presence here has already caused much disturbance. My son and I will continue the search when you have gone."

She swept away, leaving Lord Tancred openmouthed and the twins looking at each other with slight smiles of relief.

"Father," said Cassie, laying her hand on his tense fist. "It looks as if we shall never find the Shield. You must resign yourself to that. The goddess, if she's been watching us, will know we've done our best."

For a moment defiance flared in Tancred's eyes. "Well," he said, giving his children a stern look, "we still have three days. Let's not give up yet."

"I'm going to look for Will first," Keiron said determinedly. "Come on, Cassie."

They left their father to brood about the apparent failure of their mission. But his belief in historical documents, legends, maps and codes being that much stronger than immediate experience, he retired at once to the palace's dusty archives, hoping forlornly that in the little time remaining to him on the island he might find there a vital clue to the Shield's whereabouts.

It is ironic that when they all felt in their hearts that they would never find the Shield, its discovery was almost upon them.

CHAPTER 9

Crowds from the city had milled around the palace walls during the last few days, waiting for some weakening of its defences, anxious about the water supply; but as soon as the water in the Sacred Spring began to flow again, they formed into queues at the water distribution points. Wisely, and not without an inward struggle, the Queen had taken the advice of the captain of the scorpion-guards and ordered double rations of water for everyone.

Any hint of rebellion soon fizzled out.

The lizard-people arrived in the city from the Lizard Caverns too late to exploit the unrest. Dispersing in groups around the city, they stayed with sympathizers or took up residence in empty houses, waiting to see what was going to happen. For their sixth sense told them that *something* was going to happen soon, something so original, so transforming, they had to be there to take part in it.

Justus joined one of the parties; he judged that the twins were as safe in the palace as anywhere and did not need him now. He would have liked to have been with them both, never having had human friends before; but the pull of his kind was more powerful. In the excitement it had been forgotten by most that he should still be confined to the caverns. In fact, when the lizard-people saw how the scorpion-guards left him alone, in their eyes it confirmed his status as a leader-in-waiting, and they treated him with a greater deference.

Tornius, in another part of the city, was told of how Justus had disobeyed his order to stay in the caverns, but he read the minds of his followers and said nothing. This was not the time to snub the boy; there would be plenty of opportunities for that in the future.

The only sounds in the palace gardens now were the cicadas, the birds and the flow of the spring and the fountains.

The twins trailed around the vast gardens calling Will's name. They passed near the fountain where he was still stuck; but, after a night of fretting, he had fallen asleep, and he did not hear them. Then, mid-morning, a large bird, busy repairing its nest, espied what looked like a twig stuck in the top of the fountain. It settled on the rim of the disc over which the water flowed, waded across to the twig and gave it a vicious tug.

It was fortunate that the twins were near the fountain. They heard the bird splashing about in the water, and because they could not see it, they became curious.

The bird gave a final tug and pulled Will out of the pipe. Will was faint with pain, but he struggled in its beak for all he was worth. The bird rose a few feet, flapping its wings wildly, and the twins caught a glimpse of what it held. Will gave a final twist of his body before he passed out; but it was enough to free him, and he fell back into the water. The bird, alarmed at the shouting of the twins below, gave up and flew off.

"He's up there!" Keiron declared, his eyes bright with hope. "Come on, we've got to get up there."

The fountain was taller than a palm tree. It was difficult to climb: the water cascaded all over them, the discs were slippery with green slime, and the structure, made of some light metal, bent and shifted under their weight. The higher they climbed, the more precarious it felt – the fountain swayed and creaked – but that didn't stop them. They reached the top disc and gripped it, panting. It was the smallest of the discs and slippery with slime.

By now the fountain was making ominous creaking sounds above the gushing of the water; it felt very unsteady. "It's not safe," Cassie shouted above the noise. "I think I ought to go down."

But Keiron wasn't paying any attention. He was peering over the top disc. "Look," he shouted. "There he is!" He wriggled up until half his body was over the top disc.

"Be careful," said Cassie, afraid that he would slip.

Keiron's hand was within a few inches of Will, when there came a loud crack. Something gave way in the main stem of the fountain. It buckled slowly to one side, making the most hideous sounds.

Almost in slow motion, they collapsed in a heap of metal and water and slime. As they neared the ground, they let go of the fountain and tumbled down, knocking the wind out of themselves.

There was Will, floating in one of the pools of gathering water.

Keiron snatched him up. He was quite inert. Keiron shook him and called his name. He pressed the manikin against his face, then looked at Cassie, aghast. "I think he's... I think... Oh, Cassie, he's not...?" He held Will out to his sister in the palm of his hand. The manikin was limp and broken, one thin arm hung by a fibre; there was a crack in the bark around his middle and gashes in his side where the bird had pecked him. Keiron went white and his hand trembled.

Cassie lifted Will into her hand.

"He's dead, isn't he?" Keiron whispered, trying to hold back a sob. "And you're not allowed to bring dead people back to life, are you."

"Not if they have a soul," said Cassie.

"Does he have one, then?" Keiron asked.

Cassie thought hard. "Remember when I brought him alive? He was just a bit of carved wood, then. I stroked him, I felt the power go down my fingers, and then he just sprang up with that grin on his face. Well, isn't this the same?"

They looked at each other.

"Are you sure?" Keiron asked. He knew how deeply seared she had been by bringing the Child back from death, and by all the evil that had flowed from that.

"Only humans have souls," Cassie said, remembering one of her father's early lessons. "And though Will might act in some ways like us..." She shrugged her shoulders, as if her point was too evident to spell out.

She closed her eyes and stroked the manikin. The familiar and mysterious life-force coursed through her fingers into his tiny body, mending his wounds and tears. Within a minute, he jerked up into a sitting position as if he had received an electric shock, a startled look on his little green face. His eyes, once glazed and dull, now glowed, two sharp pricks of astounded light.

"Will!" Keiron shouted, snatching him from his sister's hand. "Are you all right?"

Yes, I am, he said, surprised. Then, remembering what had happened to him, he changed his mind. *No, I'm not. I'm very wet and very tired. You took your time, didn't you?*

Keiron hugged him until he protested that the life was being squeezed out of him; then the boy put the little manikin in his hair to rest.

Cassie looked at her hands and smiled: where did this mysterious healing power come from?

She looked at the damage they had done to the fountain and wondered what the Queen's reaction to it would be. She hadn't seen any scorpion-guards or gardeners around – they were all either up at the Sacred Spring, cleaning it up after the mess the Child had made of it, or supervising the water distribution outside; so perhaps the Queen wouldn't instantly know about this.

She tried to tidy up the wreck of the fountain, so that it might not look so terrible. She came across the top disc, the smallest one. Like all the others, it was covered with a crust of hard grey-green residue, overlaid with long tendrils of slimy weed. Most of the other discs were dented or buckled but this one was still a perfect circle. As she was about to lean it against the stone base of the fountain, a tiny flash of brilliant light glittered momentarily on its rim. She lifted it and slowly turned the disc, looking for the source of that light: and there it was, a little chip in the verdigris, revealing...

"Keiron," she screamed, hardly daring to believe what she might be holding in her hands.

"What?" he said, galvanized by her scream.

"Look!" She pointed with a trembling finger at the tiny glitter of gold.

After an astounded minute, his eyes wide with hope and disbelief, he said, "It isn't, is it?"

"But it can't be," said Cassie, hardly daring to believe it herself.

"We've got to chip off this hard covering," Keiron answered in a shaky voice.

They found some sharp stones. The verdigris on the metal disc, made largely of chalk and the deposits of dead weeds, soon cracked under their careful blows. They eased up the first large fragment. Underneath it there shone, unblemished, a smooth, cool surface of gold. In the gold was etched what looked like part of a map.

The twins stared and stared, then laughed hysterically as the truth could no longer be doubted. They dropped their stones and danced around, hands clasped, whooping and shrieking: it was impossible, unbelievable. They had found the Golden Shield!

"Well done, Will," Keiron shouted, holding up the manikin. "If you hadn't got stuck up there, we'd never have found it."

Then they began chipping furiously at the rest of the covering; it came away easily enough. When the last piece was removed, they picked up the Shield and carefully sluiced it in the still flowing water. It shone and glittered like a dazzling mirror

"It's amazing," said Keiron. He slipped his hand in the grip at the back of it and held it up before him like a warrior.

"It's so beautiful," said Cassie, careful not to let it blind her with the sunlight glancing off it.

A wild goose chase, Will said ruefully. *I was certainly right about that.*

They placed it carefully on the grass again and studied it. In the centre of it was a jewel-like lizard, emeralds for its eyes, sequins for its body. An outline map of the island covered most of the Shield. It showed the coast, the rocks beyond the coast that kept out travellers, the undersea volcano to the east. The main landmarks were drawn on it: the Palace of the Fountains, the city, the Sacred Spring, the oases in the deserts, the lizard-people's Underground Caverns, the Ruined City, the Lizard Ring, the Cave Dwellings, the harbours and fishing villages. And round the edge was an unbroken ring of symbols that looked vaguely familiar.

Lying flat on the grass, squinting at the shield's edge, Cassie said, "You can just see it."

"What?"

"That inner glow the Golden Armour always has. Even in this light. Look."

Keiron straightened out and squinted along the edge too. "I can see it!" he exclaimed. He lifted his gaze and grinned at his sister. "We did it, Cass," he laughed. "All three of us."

They were so full of excitement and self-congratulation, they failed to notice the Queen standing on the roof. She had heard Keiron's laughter, and the tone of it made her look with greater attention at what they were doing. For a moment she was outraged at the collapse of the fountain, and was about to storm down and give the twins such a telling off as they would never forget, when she paused. Why were they so excited about that disc? The smallest one? It looked so like...

She drew in a hissing breath and for a moment her body went rigid. *They have found the Shield*. She did not dare believe it at first, it seemed too fantastic; but as she watched with intense excitement from the very edge of the roof, she saw Keiron hold up the disc. It flashed great golden sunrays. There was no doubt about it. She barely suppressed a fierce impulse to scream triumphantly: her long nails bit into her palms and her eyes closed in ecstasy. *They had found it*. Now *she*, not the lizard-people, had the Shield. Her dynasty was safe.

"Fetch that Shield," she commanded, and four scorpion-guards swooped down from the roof

Will saw them coming first. *Look out!*

Keiron looked up, startled. The scorpion-guards' wings whirred above them and their claws reached towards them.

"Quick, Cass," Keiron shouted, clasping the Shield to his chest, ducking and swerving rapidly away from the scorpion-guards. He raced towards the palace, thinking that if he could give it to his father, it might be all right. Cassie was hard on his heels as they ran towards a back entrance. But more scorpion-guards appeared and swarmed around them angrily. It was hopeless.

"Father, help us," Cassie shouted.

"Give us the Shield," said one of the scorpion-guards, clacking his claws impatiently.

The twins clung together, loath to give up the Shield, feeling the unfairness of it, yet terrified of the waving antennae, the red-rimmed eyes, the rippling manes of the scorpion-guards.

"We shall give you a light sting," said one, stepping forward, "which will leave you in agony for days. Is that what you would like?"

"You wouldn't dare!" Keiron shouted.

"We have our orders."

Suddenly their father and the Queen appeared in the doorway. She flashed him a threatening glance, and Tancred said to his childen, "Well done, both of you. How you did it..." and he shrugged his shoulders. "But you must give it up."

"Father!" they both protested, holding fast to the Shield, yet knowing they had no choice.

"I'm sorry."

They could tell by the look on his face how infuriated he was, and that made them feel a little better. Grudgingly, Keiron let go of the Shield and dropped it at his feet. "Take it, then," he shouted sullenly.

The Queen motioned to one of the scorpion-guards, who jumped forward, seized the Shield, and presented it to her. She received it with huge satisfaction. Slipping it on her arm, she held it up and slowly revolved a full circle, as if displaying her spoils to the four corners of her kingdom. This was a great day in her life, perhaps even greater than the birth of her only son.

"Much good it will do you," Tancred muttered.

"On the contrary," she flashed back. "This removes the one possible threat to my power." She turned to re-enter the palace. "I take it you will be leaving soon, Lord Tancred, now that your mission is done."

"But the Shield..." he protested.

"Is *mine!*" she flung back triumphantly. "It is nothing more to do with you." She swept inside, a swarm of excited scorpion-guards in her wake.

The twins and their father wandered disconsolately in the garden, wondering what to do next.

"It's my fault," Keiron muttered several times, castigating himself. "I should have kept a look-out for her."

"It's no one's fault," Cassie protested.

"We could have hidden it and smuggled it out when we left," Keiron retorted hotly.

"Now, children!" Tancred said. "What's done is done. We have to think." They came to a bench against the outer wall and thankfully sat on it. "What did the goddess want us to do with it here? Before we leave?" he asked.

"That's simple," said Cassie. "Make rain."

"Of course. But how?"

The twins looked at him blankly, and shrugged. They were hoping he would be able to tell them that.

"And that, of course," he added quietly, "is precisely what the Queen *doesn't* want."

Keiron was still blaming himself. "I thought, once we had found the Shield, our troubles would be over," he complained. "When really they have only got worse."

Cassie nodded glumly. The unfairness of it all burnt in her chest.

Seeing the look on their faces, Tancred drew them to him and comforted them. "You've done what you came here for, you've found the Shield. It is out in the open at last, just as it should be. Now we shall see how its power, which the goddess gave it so long ago, will manifest itself. Brace yourself for difficult – and exciting – times ahead, my children. We won't be leaving quite yet."

The Queen was only too aware of the potential danger the Shield posed to her: if it brought rain, her power would slip away. Who would need her, or her Sacred Spring then? There would be a power struggle between the scorpion-guards and the lizard-people, and she would be swept aside whoever won. No, she had no choice but to destroy the Shield. Her life, her dynasty, depended on it.

But not yet. It had existed for centuries in the mythology of the island, as its central mystery. Books had been written about it, theories expounded as to its whereabouts, reputations built upon and ruined by it, art and stories created out of it, lives destroyed in the eternal hunt for it. And at last, she, of all their race and history, was the one to possess it. What an extraordinary and distinguishing fact! It had to be recorded in history. No, she could not bring herself to destroy it just yet; first, everyone should know that she possessed it.

She brought the Shield down to the throne room and placed it on her late husband's empty throne. "There," she whispered to his memory. "What do you think of your Queen now?" But the Shield seemed to wink back at her mockingly, reflecting the light from the roof windows.

She called a servant. "See that a proper stand is made for it," she ordered.

By the end of the day, the Shield hung, suspended like a gong. In the dim light of the vast throne room, it glowed softly. The Queen sat broodingly for hours on her throne, contemplating it. What was its secret?

Word soon spread in the city that the Queen had found the Golden Shield. Crowds gathered around the palace walls, among them the lizard-people.

"We must get it from her," Tornius fumed, beside himself with fear and envy.

The lizard-people tried to invade the palace but they suffered several casualties within the first few minutes. They were not strong enough on their own. The rest of the populace were little more than curious bystanders, waiting for some miracle; they were not willing to join them in battle.

"I shall go in alone, then," said Tornius. "I shall try to sneak into the palace and steal the Shield. They will hardly be expecting that." Several of his closest advisers cautioned against this. "What choice do we have?" he said. "The scorpion-guards won't dare touch me. I survived their Sting, remember. The rest of you wouldn't stand a chance in there."

"Then take Justus with you," they answered. "They won't dare touch him, either."

Tornius's eyes darkened a little. He hesitated a long time. In that time he felt first a surge of jealous impatience: he had not yet got used to the fact that someone else now shared his special status. This was countered by the more noble thought that his race needed to have a successor waiting in the wings; but if the boy was killed or captured... His shook his head vigorously, as if to free them of these troublesome thoughts. "Let him come, then," he said grudgingly. "Though what a mere boy can do..." He shrugged his shoulders with light contempt.

Justus was sent for. He felt the honour of being chosen for this mission. He sensed Tornius's mistrust and ambivalence too: maybe this would be the time to prove himself in the eyes of his leader; for he knew that he needed that approval if his position wasn't to be constantly undermined in the future. And he was pleased to be given the chance of seeing his friends the twins again, too.

He led Tornius along the same route he had taken before, slithering through the undergrowth and into the water under the arch where the Spring flowed into the garden. They watched for a while the comings and goings in the garden. "Only scorpion-guards," Tornius said. "They're no threat to us. But it would be easier if we could get into the palace unnoticed."

"If I could only attract the children's attention," Justus said, "they would let us in."

"You'll do as I say," Tornius said curtly. "Just keep behind me and do as I do. Is that understood?"

Justus sighed inwardly.

But Tornius wasn't really thinking of the boy at that moment. The thought of the Shield, and its close proximity, preoccupied him: *he was near to possessing it.*

If the legends were right – and why shouldn't they be? – the Shield would bring rain to his burning country; it would save his race. The only thing that stood between that triumph and himself was the Queen. His hatred for her burned like an ember in his eyes. Justus looked into them and was afraid.

Out in the desert, Badrur sat on his camel in the fierce heat, looking back at the Child in deep exasperation. She had been in a skittish mood from the moment she had followed him across the stony desert, forever stopping to rest, or play in the sand, or chase his Salamander, or doze. They had not got far, certainly not far enough away from the palace for him to abandon her in the hope that she would get lost and die in the sandy wastes; indeed, he could still see the city shimmering like a mirage on the horizon, and he longed to be rid of this monster, that he might return to civilization after the weeks spent in the wild.

But for once the delay worked to his advantage. A flying scorpion-guard, sent by the Queen to bring him back, alighted in front of his camel and gave him the news. He could hardly believe it at first, and questioned the guard closely. Then, at last convinced, he punched the air in a silent gesture of triumph; he wanted to cry victory over the empty landscape too, but he held back for fear of waking the Child.

Turning his Great Salamander, he spurred it into a fast trot, leaving the Child to stir and dribble in her dark dreams. He would have the Shield for himself, whatever his mother might wish.

* * *

The Queen studied the map and the runes on the Shield for many hours that night before she would admit that she could not fathom its secret. How could such a thing bring rain? But she was no longer sure she should destroy it. Wouldn't the people revere her more if they knew she was the keeper of the Shield? As long as no one penetrated its secret, she would be safe. No one, that is, except herself. She and her descendants must know its secret; and the people must know that she – and in time her son – was the guardian of that secret. Then her power to control the flow of water would be both mystical and beyond challenge.

In the morning, she called Lord Tancred and his children into the throne room. Perhaps they could unravel its mystery. If they did, she could always have them killed, once she knew its secret.

The twins sat either side of the Shield on the dusty floor. They were glad to see it again; they felt that its glow cast a protective spell over them.

Their father and the Queen talked for some time about the markings on the Shield. Then Tancred drew from his pocket a little notebook. The twins recognized it as the one they had picked up after his accident in the ruined city. In it they had copied down the symbols that were scratched on the inside rim of the dried up well; he had soon noticed that they were identical to the ones on the rim of the Shield. Documents in the Archives had helped him decipher the message; now he judged the time was ripe to reveal it.

He showed her the symbols in his notebook, told her where they came from and how they matched those on the Shield. She looked startled.

"This is how I translate them," he said. *"When the leader strikes me, before the rain falls, the walls of tyranny will crumble, and you shall be free."*

There was a silence while they repeated this to themselves, considering it.

"How noble," said the Queen, her lip curling in sarcasm. "A riddle! Am I meant to be impressed by that?"

"You will make of it what you will," said Tancred.

"You disappoint me, Lord Tancred, if that's the best you can do." She paused. "Have you no notion of what it means?"

But he wasn't going to help her out. He could see that the words disturbed her, as he had intended, and that pleased him.

She rose to go, steely contempt in her eyes. "Your purpose in coming here is fulfilled. You should make your preparations to leave."

Tancred stepped back formally and gave an ironic bow. "Yes, I am conscious that we have overstayed our welcome." Then he added with apparent off-handedness, "We do, of course, intend to take the Shield with us. The goddess Citatha expects it of us."

"Never!" she cried, suddenly losing her self-control. *"Never!* The Shield is mine. Now leave me," she screamed. "Get out!"

"Madam," Tancred protested.

"If you haven't left by dawn tomorrow," she hissed, her dark eyes blazing, her hands curling and uncurling, "I shall let the scorpions do with you what they have been longing to do ever since you came. *Sting you to death!"*

CHAPTER 10

The twins spent the rest of that uncomfortable day in the Archives with their father, trying to work out how the Shield could bring rain to the island. The map on the Shield compared well with ancient drawings of it on some crumbling scrolls he had dug out of a cupboard: it showed the ruined city as the once thriving centre of the island; there was the Sacred Spring but no palace and only a small settlement around it; and there were many more oases in the deserts. But no clues as to how to release its rain-making powers.

Were there incantations to be said over it? They hunted for these, and having found some in a large old book, they recited the more likely ones; but nothing happened. "Perhaps we have to say them over the Shield itself," said Tancred.

"It was easy with the Golden Helmet," Cassie sighed. "We just had to put it on."

"Why does the goddess make everything such a riddle?" Keiron wondered. "Why can't she just tell us what to do?"

"We'd just be her puppets, then," Tancred answered.

"Sometimes I wouldn't mind that," said Cassie.

"I think," said Tancred, "that her magic works through our free will. Through the choices we make and the courage we show. That's why she doesn't give us the answers. We have to solve the riddles ourselves, then her magic can work."

When evening fell, the twins left their father to it and went up on to the roof. The breeze was cooling and the moon was rising above the desert horizon. Lights flickered in the city, and there seemed much toing and froing beyond the walls, but the air was calmer. They sat there for a while, listening to the comforting flow of the spring, watching the stars come out, swatting the insects that buzzed around them, yet thinking how glad they were to be leaving this place.

"Do you feel homesick?" Cassie asked.

Keiron traced a circle in the sand on the flat roof while he considered this. "Right now, I'd give a lot to be able to roll around in a heap of snow," he laughed. "But no, not really. I like travelling, discovering new places, however horrible some of them turn out to be. How about you?"

Whenever Cassie thought of North Island, the succession of mental pictures always froze at Tara's grave. It was a beautiful place in the wood, a mound of flowers tended by the wolf-people, but it had a biting sadness. She shook her head. "I wonder where we'll go next?" she said.

"Back to Temple Island, I suppose."

"With or without the Shield?"

"With it, of course," he exclaimed; how could she doubt it?

They fantasized how they might trick the scorpion-guards, seize the Shield and escape with it down the long tunnel to the Cave Dwellings, there to release its secret and bring rain to the land. Such dreams did not have much practical use but they kept their spirits up.

They were disturbed by noises in the garden. A voice shouted, "Stop! You!"

They knew that voice only too well. So he was back. Badrur!

They peered over the roof edge.

In the shadowy garden below there were three figures, dark and silvered in the moonlight: Badrur, and two lizard-people.

Keiron clutched Cassie. "Isn't that Justus?" he whispered.

They could just make out the distinctive pattern on their friend's skin. "I think it is," Cassie whispered back, alarmed. "He said he would return, didn't he."

"Who's the other one?"

Cassie waited until the moonlight fell full on the other one's face. "It's Tornius, the leader of the lizard-people. I told you about him."

"Stand and fight," Badrur was shouting. "Or creep away like the dogs you are."

They heard Tornius telling Justus to get away, but the lizard-boy simply fell back a little. "Go," Tornius hissed. He knew instinctively that he would not survive this encounter. Justus was the heir, he must go, that's all that mattered. He now understood why Justus had survived the Sting and he regretted all his petty jealousies and unworthy thoughts in the face of that overwhelming fact.

Why doesn't Justus run? Keiron said to Will. *He doesn't stand a chance against Badrur.*

He wouldn't know how to, not when his leader's in danger. They're one big family, remember.

Suddenly, a trail of glistening venom snaked from Tornius's mouth. The prince neatly side-stepped it. Justus hurled venom too but it fell just short. Before either of them could gather enough venom for a second shot, Badrur was upon Tornius. There was a fierce thrashing wrestle, so vicious and fast-moving, all Justus could do was leap about, vainly looking for a way to help his leader.

The two broke apart, panting. As they glared at each other, they knew they were equal in strength and cunning. But Badrur had one advantage, and he chose this moment to use it. His eyes suddenly glowed in the dark, signalling their hypnotic power. Tornius resisted it at once, but the energy and attention needed for that weakened and distracted him at this crucial moment, and Badrur pounced on him.

The twins' hearts were in their mouths. The grunts and hissings and shrieks from the lizard made their skin prickle. That horrible feeling of dark dismay that comes when, against hope and expectation, one's own side, one's hero, is inevitably failing, stole over them, until neither could bear to look. They hid their eyes and missed the final moment.

Badrur had his foot on the lizard's neck. They heard a loud crack.

Looking up, they saw Justus hurl himself at the bloodied prince. But one expert blow knocked the lizard-boy sideways. He convulsed on the grass and then went still. Badrur gave him one contemptuous kick, wiped the blood from his hands on his robe and strode into the palace, well satisfied with this little diversion. If he had known just who he had killed – the leader of the enemy – he might have lingered over his triumph, perhaps brought his mother out to witness it, and he would have felt a much deeper sense of satisfaction too. And if he had known that Justus was the heir, he'd not have been so content with that last kick either.

The twins watched Justus anxiously for any signs of life. He did not move.

A couple of scorpion-guards appeared and approached the bodies.

"I'm going down," said Cassie, "before they take Justus away. He might still be alive."

They got there just as the scorpion-guards were lifting him.

"He's alive," Keiron shouted at them; because of the taboo on touching a live lizard that had survived the sting, the scorpion-guards dropped him like a hot brick.

"Please let him live," Cassie said to herself as she knelt beside the body. She knew nothing about the anatomy of lizard-people, but she felt over him, looking for a pulse, not knowing where the pressure points were. Keiron joined in too.

"He *is* dead," said one of the scorpion-guards, beginning to think the children were trying to trick them. "Like the other one."

"He is not!" they protested.

Let me try, said Will. The manikin stretched out on

Justus's chest and put his tiny ear against the cold, scaly skin. He felt the faint vibrations of a just-beating heart. *Yes!*

"He's alive, Cassie. Quick."

She laid her hands on his head and moved slowly down, feeling for injuries. But there was only one, a crack in the skull where Badrur had hit him, and one bruise where he had been kicked. Under her hands, she felt the bruise dissolve, the crack fuse and the damage to his brain heal.

With a shudder, Justus came to. He sat up, his eyes bright with fear. In a second, he took in all that had happened. "Where is he?" he hissed angrily, looking around for Badrur.

"He's gone inside," said Keiron. "Cassie saved your life."

"Again?" he said, turning to her, suddenly abashed. He took her hand in his cold claw, and was about to pour out his gratitude when he saw the scorpion-guards lifting Tornius's body. He drew in a sharp breath. "Don't let them take him," he cried out urgently. "He must be buried in the proper way."

He slithered over to the scorpion-guards and gave them such a threatening look, they dropped Tornius and drew back. He looked at the corpse of his leader with sadness: throughout his childhood, Tornius had been the one he had looked up to, feared and respected; he had seemed invincible. And the coldness, the unfairness, Tornius had lately treated him with, all that was now forgotten. This was a sad day for his people.

Justus might not have felt quite the same if he knew what murderous thoughts Tornius had occasionally harboured against him these last few days; but that was a secret Tornius took to his grave.

"Help me to lift him," he implored the twins.

They lifted the limp and heavy body across the grass and into the bushes. At the arch over the Spring, they rested.

"I'll carry him to my people in the city," Justus said. "The scorpion-guards won't dare to try and stop me."

He took Cassie's hand again and she looked into his liquid eyes. "I thank you again, Cassie. You are a true sister to me, heart and soul."

"Won't we see you again?" she said, caught unawares by such an abrupt farewell. "We're being forced to leave tomorrow."

"Then I will come back. I shan't be long. I have a feeling, anyway, that there are still many things to happen before you will be allowed to leave."

Me too, said Will, perched on Keiron's shoulder.

Justus gave Keiron a quick hug. "We'll be on the roof, then," Keiron whispered. "We'll keep a look-out for you."

They helped him hitch Tornius's dead body on to his shoulders. He shuffled forward towards the city, scorpion-guards buzzing warily around him, the heavy burden of his leader's body on his back. It was for the twins an unforgettable image, a dead leader being carried back to his people by the young pretender.

The twins heard voices in the throne room and crept unnoticed through the shadows to listen. The Queen and Prince Badrur sat on their thrones while Lord Tancred paced back and forth in front of them. The

Golden Shield glowed softly on its stand, the emerald of the lizard's eye watching them as if it was alive.

Argument raged between the three adults. Tancred put forward the spiritual history of the Shield, its origins and purpose: he insisted that it had to go back to Temple Island. But then it might bring rain, the Queen countered icily. Tancred tried in vain to make them see that, if the Shield was capable of doing that, as the goddess intended, then it was right and proper that rain should fall. That enraged the Queen, for it spelt death to her dynasty; and in this she was backed up by her son. He, however, wanted the Shield for himself, something to accompany him on his travels, like a trophy; having been cheated of the Helmet, this was doubly important to him. So the argument, a tangle of conflicting fears and desires, raged on.

"Let's go up to the roof again," Cassie whispered, wearying of all this talk.

Much later that night, when the inhabitants of the palace were sleeping, Justus returned. Briefly, he whispered of the sorrow among his people at Tornius's death. He seemed somewhat distracted, and the twins guessed his people had already impressed on him that he would soon be made the next leader. It was an awesome thought for anyone, let alone one so young, however much in theory it had been expected. But there was no time to think about that, they still had to rescue the Shield.

They stole into the sleeping palace and up to the deserted throne room.

There they read the inscription around the Shield to Justus: he grew very excited about that, then awed. *When the leader strikes me, before the rain falls, the walls of tyranny will crumble, and you shall be free.* He chanted that to himself like a mantra until its sense threatened to disintegrate with repetition.

"What is it, Justus?" Cassie asked, seeing how troubled he was.

"I may have been named as leader of the lizard-people," he said. "But I have not yet been through the proper ceremony. Should *I* then strike the Shield? And if I did, what would happen?"

"The walls of tyranny would crumble," Keiron quoted.

"And what are the walls of tyranny?" Justus asked softly.

"You mean – the palace?" Cassie asked, suddenly grasping the truth. "The palace walls will crumble?"

Justus nodded. "Why not?"

"I don't understand," said Keiron. The thought of the palace crumbling before their eyes was so fantastical that for a while the twins refused to entertain it seriously. And anyway, how could the Shield make that happen?

Even Justus began to look doubtful.

"Let's ask Father," said Cassie.

They found their father sitting on his bed, deep in troubled thought, his scanty belongings packed.

"Ah," he said. "You could not sleep either. Well, it is not surprising, and it is just as well. Dawn will soon be here..."

"Father," Cassie interrupted him. "Justus thinks he knows what the message on the Shield means."

Lord Tancred listened to the strange lizard-boy, with his youthful human face and prehistoric body, and it came to him that this was the sign he had been waiting for. The goddess did not do things by half-measures. If the Helmet could transform North Island into a paradise in the space of an hour, then the Shield might well be able to bring down the walls of the Queen's palace.

Tancred laid his hand on the lizard-boy's shoulders and said, "Justus, I believe the goddess has chosen you to perform the first of the Shield's acts. Come, let us not delay any longer."

In the vast Throne Room, the Shield glowed brighter than ever, a soft vibration of light. It was suspended in its stand like a gong.

"If Justus does succeed in this," said Keiron, still doubting that he would, "what about all the servants? Shouldn't we warn them?"

Tancred shook his head, implacable. "They chose to ally themselves with the Queen. They didn't have to, she didn't force them to; and anyway, if they returned to the city they would probably be hounded or killed as collaborators. No, if they lived by the Queen, they must die by her."

Cassie shivered at this harsh judgement, but this wasn't the time to question it. For a moment, her father reminded her of Tornius, and it gave her a new light to view him by, one which did not make her feel quite comfortable. But after all, she thought, they are – or were – both leaders.

Justus ran his hands over the rim of the Shield, reading the message for himself. Now he felt sure it was for him. "I am ready," he said, solemnly.

"If nothing happens," said Cassie. "Don't be too disappointed. It'll just mean..." But at a withering look from her friend, her voice trailed away. "Have faith, Cassie," was all he said.

"This is dangerous for us, too," said Tancred. "Before Justus strikes the Shield, we must be sure of our escape. I propose..."

"The tunnel!" Keiron cried. "The one under the palace that leads to the Cave Dwellings. That'll be our escape route."

Lord Tancred agreed. "Yes, we can't rely on the scorpion-guards to leave us alone once they see their world under attack. The tunnel's our best choice."

"Then we'll need food and water," said Cassie.

Justus sighed at the delay, but he knew it was necessary. The twins fetched food from the kitchen and filled water-bottles, and brought them back to the Throne Room.

"Now we are ready," said Tancred to Justus.

This was the lizard-boy's supreme moment. He wasn't nervous, just anxious to acquit himself well for his race. He positioned himself at right-angles to the Shield.

"Go to the entrance," he said, and the others moved away, ready to dart down the stairs to the tunnel door at the first sign of danger.

Justus, now a proud and lonely creature under the great dome of the Throne Room, lifted his powerful tail and swung it back and forth, gathering momentum. Then he stepped closer to the Shield and hit it as hard as he could with his swinging tail.

The Shield emitted a deep, booming note like a

powerful gong. The note trembled at first as the Shield swung on its stand, then settled into a sound that resonated and swelled. Justus did not have to hit it again: the sound appeared to feed on its own mysterious energy and grew louder and louder. It became a deep, penetrating boom.

Boooohm. . .

Justus crouched on all fours and watched the Shield grow luminous in the vibrating gloom. He was amazed and frightened by the power one blow of his tail had unleashed.

The *boooohm* of the vibrating note filled the vast dome and vibrated through its wall into other rooms, down passages and stairs. Its volume gathered, deepened, penetrated. When the leader of the lizard-people struck the Shield, an ancient power had been unleashed. It vibrated destructively in every molecule in the palace walls, floors, pillars, arches and ceilings, destabilizing internal structures and causing atoms to collide. The palace began to shake from within to its very foundations.

The *boooohm* swelled and swelled.

"Come on, Justus," the twins cried, brick dust beginning to fall into their hair.

"The Shield!" Tancred cried, running forward.

He lifted it on its stand and staggered with it across the shifting Throne Room and down the stairs. All about them, walls were cracking, stones disintegrating, dust cascading. At the bottom of the stairs, the floor of the passage to the tunnel door suddenly split with a giant zig-zag, and they had to press against the trembling wall as they hurried along.

They reached the tunnel doorway and put the Shield down. Its *boooohm* was relentless. They stared at it with awe: how could something so small produce such a powerful and far-reaching sound? From above came the sound of plates and mirrors crashing to the floor, ornaments shattering. They heard the cries of the servants and the shrieks of scorpion-guards. The twins, feeling their own bodies shaking, vainly blocked their ears.

Justus felt exultation bubbling up inside him. It was working: by his own efforts, he had destroyed the citadel of tyranny.

There was a louder noise, as of a wall or a pillar collapsing.

"This is incredible," said Tancred. "It's like a massive earthquake."

"It's a terrible revenge," said Justus. "I did not think the Shield could be so powerful."

"The whole place will crumble to dust," said Tancred. "But we can't stop to watch. Come on. Let's get out of here before this tunnel entrance caves in too."

"But we can't go in there," said Justus, pointing to the tunnel, "until the Shield is silent again. Otherwise, it might destroy the tunnel too." So they were forced to wait at the tunnel entrance, listening to the Palace of the Fountains disintegrate above them.

The palace was imploding. The Shield had begun its work.

When the first deep boom had sounded through the palace, Badrur was smoking one of his beloved hookahs, re-living in a dreamy state the pleasure of killing the lizard-man. He stiffened in surprise. Hookahs and jars began to vibrate, and bottles shattered on the floor. Was this an earthquake? There had often been earth tremors – but that booming sound, what was that? It penetrated everything.

He ran into the passage. Already dust was falling, and little cracks were appearing in the brickwork. He stood irresolutely and felt the whole building shudder. The mysterious *booooohm* grew louder. His one thought then was to save his own skin: if this was an earth tremor, he had to get out quickly.

But the Shield? He hesitated. *He must have it!*

He raced down the stairs. The *boooohm* sounded, the walls shook, and when he entered the dome, the thrones were shaking on their dais.

The Shield had gone!

Furiously, he thought his mother must have taken it.

But what *was* that booming?

Suddenly, there was a loud crack above him. A long split, the shape of a bolt of lightning, shivered across the dome. Dust cascaded over his head. There was no time to lose.

He leapt down the main stairway two or three steps at a time, to the main entrance. Just as he got there, the ceiling of the entrance hall caved in. Covered in brick dust, he retreated to the landing, cursing. Everything was collapsing around him. Why? And what should he do?

He closed his eyes and called telepathically for his Great Salamander. If he could get to the roof, the creature would lift him free.

As he climbed through the palace, he felt the great edifice, the place that had been his home from infancy, shifting and tilting and groaning like a building caught in a hurricane. Bricks broke loose and shattered, pillars snapped, floors split, ceilings caved in. There was no time for regrets; with the agility of a cat, he dodged every missile, ever leaping upwards.

On the top floor, he saw his mother. She was at the end of a long passage, covered in white brick dust: she looked like a ghost. She held out her hands towards him and cried out; he hesitated. Would he have gone forward to try and save her, or have run on to save his own skin first? Neither ever knew, for at that moment the ceiling caved in and she disappeared in a cloud of dust and rubble.

He struggled on to the roof.

The whole palace was juddering now, and the flat roof was a maze of cracks and gaping black holes.

He watched as the palace garden walls crumbled too, but curiously, none of the buildings beyond the walls seemed affected. How could this be if this was an earthquake?

And that *boooohm*: what *was* it? He thought his head might burst with the sound of it.

The roof shifted beneath his feet and he leapt to one side just in time to avoid being swallowed up by a hole. There wasn't much time.

Then the Great Salamander burst through the garden's collapsing walls and pounded over towards its master. Badrur leapt on its neck with only a moment to spare. He looked down on the palace roof and saw the whole lot implode in a cloud of dust.

Had his mother survived that? It seemed unlikely. If that was the case, he was now the king of East Island. His ascent to kingship was not quite how he imagined it would be, but it was dramatic enough! A flame of ambition and triumph flared within his heart – and then as abruptly it gutted out. What kingdom? Surrounded by a desert, a palace in ruins, and everyone an enemy. He wasn't even sure if the scorpion-guards would do his bidding, now that his mother had gone.

Pah! What did it matter? The world was a larger and richer place than this little barren island.

He turned the Great Salamander and pointed it in the direction of the Cave Dwellings. He would retreat there for a while and consider what to do.

The scorpion-guards massed in the palace gardens. They were profoundly shocked and bewildered by the collapse of their world. The city populace, who were swarming over the gardens and about the rubble, threw stones at them. It was time to leave. The wingless ones climbed on to the backs of the flying ones. They rose in a great whirring cloud and took themselves off to a remote oasis to lick their wounds.

The twins and their father trekked through the underground tunnel with the now silent Shield, wondering what new wonders and shocks it had in store for them.

"I knew certain vibrations could shatter a glass," said Keiron. "But a palace! Wow!" It didn't quite match up to the power of the Helmet, which changed the whole climate of North Island in the space of an hour or so, but it was still pretty impressive.

You've seen nothing yet! Will promised.

Why, what else do you see?

Rain! Everywhere!

Oh, I do hope so. I'm parched.

"Well, half the inscription on the Shield came true," said Cassie to Justus. "Now we have to wait for the rains to fall..."

"Then we shall be free," Justus added with a smile.

The Child was moving towards the city. Faint strains of the Shield's *booohm* had reached her ears. She felt it was calling to her. She ran towards the city shimmering on the horizon.

When she reached it, the people hid or scattered at her approach.

Where was Badrur? She stumbled about, calling again and again, "B-der", until she got tired of that. Then she came to the palace.

When she saw the ruins, she clapped her hands and laughed with glee.

She climbed about the rubble, throwing bits of it into the air, pulling out fragments of broken chairs and bed and bits of cloth. This was almost as much fun as the mud at the Spring!

And then she heard a faint cry, like a strangled bird.

She scrabbled slowly, warily, over to the sound and put her ear to some rubble. Something was trapped there! She pulled away the rubble.

An old woman blinked at her!

She squealed in surprise and drew back.

The old woman moaned and squirmed in her trap, squinting in the dazzzling light. Intrigued, the Child reached into the cavity that had been the old woman's resting place for two days. She pulled her up by her torn gown and sat her on the rubble. The old woman, weak and overwhelmed, passed out.

The Child shook her in puzzlement. Then she slung her over her shoulders and climbed down from the rubble. She remembered the Spring. That was the place to be in this blistering heat. She climbed up the bank to the Spring with the old woman lolling on her back, still unconscious.

She washed the old woman in the Sacred Spring, crooning over and stroking her as if she was a doll. The torn robe came away, its golden sequins floating and glittering on the current. She sat the old woman on the rock.

By now the old woman had come to. Her eyes were unseeing, and she half-sang, half-talked to herself, naked and wizened. She was like an old turtle deprived of its shell. The trauma of the last two days had robbed her of her sanity. She was no longer a vicious queen, she was like an innocent child again.

The Child was delighted to have someone who, as it transpired, was happy to be fed and washed by her like a baby and be taken for rides on her back.

They delighted in each other's infantile company.

Badrur sweltered on the back of his Great Salamander. Out in the desert, he remembered the Shield and cursed his haste to get away. It is somewhere in all that rubble, he thought. He had to find it: he wasn't sure how. Perhaps his monsters at the Cave Dwellings could do the excavation for him.

At least that pompous Tancred and his meddling children were dead. So much for the power of the goddess Citatha! he laughed to himself.

The world wasn't such a bad place after all, if you knew how to keep one step ahead.

But what of rain?

The Shield had unleashed some of its power, but not the most important part. The land still shrivelled slowly in the heat. The water underground and in the Lizard Caves continued to dry up. Sandstorms still howled in the desert. Oases shrank. The island continued its slow and scorching death.

Its life was in the hands of Justus, the twins, Will and their father now. But they, nearing the Cave Dwellings, tired and dusty after their long trek, were no nearer to solving the riddle of the Shield than they had ever been. Or so they thought.

CHAPTER 11

They arrived at the Cave Dwellings exhausted and thirsty. Their water bottles had run dry the day before, but their rations of food had just held out. Keiron led them straight to the well, and they sat around it, thankfully gulping down the warm and slightly bitter water. They lifted buckets of it and splashed it over one another to cool each other and to bathe. Then they raided the dried food store and chewed on wizened figs and dates.

After the twilight gloom of the tunnel, the dazzling sunlight hurt their eyes too much at first. All they could see were Badrur's monsters dozing in the heat some distance away under clumps of palm trees.

Tethered to a rail were three forlorn-looking camels. Taking pity on them, they brought them buckets of water and dried fruit.

That night Justus slept close to the Shield. He remembered waking in the night and seeing the emerald eye glowing in the Shield's lizard. In it, he saw a paradise, like a great oasis, in which lizard-children played in the cool, wet undergrowth and splashed in glittering pools.

That dream faded into another one, a darker one. He saw his own blood flow like amber-coloured rivers over the island, and whatever part of the landscape his blood touched sprang to life.

At breakfast, he told the others of these dreams; were they merely his mind projecting what he wished, or were they a kind of prophecy?

Will too had his dreams, of great tropical forests full of gaudy blooms and amphibious wildlife. On impulse, he climbed on to the Shield and slid across it to the lizard at its centre. He sat on the lizard's back. Justus swivelled round and cried out in protest; to him, this seemed sacrilegious.

Will, get off there, Keiron demanded.

Will shook his head dreamily, hardly hearing them. He stretched full length along the lizard's back and looked into its emerald eye. Forests everywhere: he saw himself climbing a long stalk, bouncing from leaf to leaf and settling inside a great yellow bloom covered in drops of rain...

Justus couldn't bear this any longer. He took a swipe at Will, to brush him aside, and then drew his hand back with a sharp hiss as if he had been stung.

Will toppled off the Shield and fell awkwardly between Justus's two hind legs. He looked up apprehensively. A drop of something wet and sticky fell on his little head. Justus's blood!

"What's happened, Justus?" Cassie asked, alarmed at the look on the lizard-boy's face.

"I cut myself on the mouth of the lizard," he said, puzzled.

Keiron took a closer look at the lizard. "Hey, that

wasn't there before," he said, pointing at the lizard's mouth. From it there now protruded a forked tongue; it had stabbed at Justus's hand deep enough to make him bleed.

Will was too frightened to move, thinking Justus would blame him for the wound. Several more drops of Justus's amber-coloured blood dripped on to him. *Help me, Keiron, will you!* he cried. But they ignored him while Cassie laid her hands on Justus's little wound and Keiron explained to his father what had happened.

That made Will furious. *How dare they treat me like this*, he thought. In a fit of defiance, he jumped back on to the Shield and ran across towards the lizard again. Behind him he left a thin trail of Justus's blood.

The emerald eye of the lizard began to glow again. Will cautiously veered to the right. He moved over the map etched on the Shield – to the picture of the Cave Dwellings.

What are you doing? Keiron hissed, suddenly noticing him.

Exploring, said Will facetiously.

You are in a funny mood. Get off there before Justus kicks you off again.

Justus saw the thin trail of blood glistening on the Shield. It reminded him of the amber-coloured rivers of blood in his dream. His eyes lit up, and his skin shivered: he felt that he was on the very brink of the Shield's secret.

Keiron lifted Will off the Shield and rinsed him in a bowl of water.

Gradually, the Shield glowed more intensely. They all watched it, gripped with a sense of expectancy.

Suddenly, there came a sound from outside that made them all start in utter disbelief. It was a sound the twins hadn't heard since they had left North Island, and it was a sound Justus had never heard, except in his deepest dreams.

Rain!

For a minute they listened to it without moving, incredulous. Then they scrambled to the cave entrance – Tancred just as excited as his children – and looked out on a sight they had hardly dared hope ever to see. Cool, clear, sunlit rain was cascading down, light and singing. It splashed and bounced off the rocks and created millions of tiny, shifting craters in the sand.

They stood on the parapet in front of the elevated cave entrances and let the water drench them. It was a marvellous, cleansing sensation: drumming on their heads, hissing in their ears, running down their bodies. The twins laughed and shouted, clapped and jumped about. Tancred closed his eyes and held up his face to the water. Justus simply stared, unable to believe what was happening; he shivered all over in delight.

"It's incredible!" Cassie shrieked.

"A sort of miracle," her father agreed.

A few minutes later, Justus and the twins climbed up to the top of the cliff, helped by the craggy surface and the tough plants that clung to its side. There, they saw a curious sight. The rain was not universal: it fell like an airborne river; either side of it, there was no rain, just burning, arid sunlight. How could that be? And why?

Will, clinging to Keiron's wet hair, had a flash of inspiration that not only explained it, but finally gave them the key to unlocking the power of the Shield. *It's just like the trail of Justus's blood I left on the Shield,* he said excitedly to Keiron.

I don't understand, said Keiron, struggling to comprehend what was happening.

But Justus did. The minute Keiron repeated what Will had said, he flashed one look of admiration at the manikin, then slithered down the cliff face as if his tail had been scalded.

He thinks it's true, said Will.

Breathlessly, Justus told Tancred of Will's "discovery", the link between the river of rain and the trail of blood on the Shield. Tancred nodded eagerly; he liked the idea of the lizard-people's "ancient blood", as he put it, providing the essential link they had been looking for.

The twins arrived, puffed out from the rapid downward climb and saturated to the skin. "It would appear," he said to them, "that Justus's blood, when applied to the Shield, activates the rain. *That is the Shield's secret.*"

Justus could hardly believe that at last he was on the threshold of all that his people had longed for, generation after generation. "But why my blood?"

"You are your people's new leader, or at least the designated one," Tancred explained. "But more than that, you have been chosen by Citatha, just as my children have. She recognizes some magical quality in you which no one else can see." He turned to the Shield. "Well, let's try it again," he said. "I'm afraid you'll need to snag your finger on the lizard's tongue again, to make the blood flow."

They watched as Justus pressed the lizard's tongue into his hand again. He winced at the pain.

"Now drip some more blood over the picture of the Cave Dwellings."

He did so: where there were only smears of his blood, left by Will, now a little pool of lizard blood covered the picture and the desert immediately around it.

They could hear the rain intensify outside. Looking out, it was like a deluge. Great sheets of water sluiced down and hissed in the sand.

"I'll go up and see if it's raining everywhere else," Justus shouted above the noise.

He could see nothing but rain from horizon to horizon, great glittering walls of it. He was glad he was alone then. This was his supreme moment. With water hissing all around him, he thumped his tail hard on the splashing rocks and felt shivers of ecstasy pass through him again and again.

For the rest of that morning they sat in the cave entrance and watched the rain thunder down. It seemed endless; but by late afternoon, it eased off a little, settling into a more gentle downpour.

With visibility better, they could see some of its immediate effects. Chief of these was the plight of Badrur's hapless monsters. The surface sand was turning to quicksand, and the monsters, bellowing and floundering, were slowly sinking into it. The flying ones had been beaten down to the ground by the force of the rain and now their great wings were heavy with wet sand: they flapped around with ever-decreasing energy; some had already expired. The fat, heavy ones were deep in the quicksand, sinking slowly to their death, while the tall, long-necked ones struggled vainly to find a firmer footing. It was a slow and horrible death. The twins could not look on it for long, but Justus seemed satisfied and watched every minute of it.

"Buried alive," Cassie shuddered.

"But you're not sorry, are you?" Keiron asked. "Not after all the damage they caused us back home."

"No, of course not."

"But, all the same, it is sad to see them perish so ignominiously," said their father. "After having been virtual fossils for so long, death by drowning, either at sea or in quicksand, was hardly a fate worth waiting for. Badrur's meddling, of course."

"The Great Salamander survives," Justus reminded them. "And I'm glad in a way."

"Why?" asked Cassie.

"The first time I saw it, I felt that it might have been one of our ancestors."

"Yes, you're right," Tancred nodded, surprised by the insight. "In fact, it's quite possible that your very race might have descended from that creature's seed. A remote possibility, perhaps, but still there."

"I think I'm glad we shall never know," said Cassie wryly.

"Where do you think Badrur is now?" Keiron wondered.

Her father shrugged. "Let's hope he's under the palace rubble. That's where he belongs."

A little later Justus said, "I want to make it rain over the whole island. I want it to rain on my people in the Lizard Caverns and on the Ruined City. Everywhere!"

They returned to the Shield.

"First, the ruined city where the Dormant Ones are," said Justus. "They have waited long enough for rain." He dripped his blood on to the icon of the ruined city etched on the Shield. "Once the rain penetrates to the buried eggs in the dome," he said, "the young lizard-people will begin to hatch. I want to see that. They are our future, and I must be there."

"Then you must go there," said Cassie. "It's not something you can miss."

Out in the central desert, dark clouds instantly massed over the ruined city. The lizard-people who were there guarding the eggs looked up in amazement. They leapt about in the rain that suddenly hissed in the sand about them, almost choking in their joy. Soon the rain would begin to seep through the cracked roof of the ancient dome beneath which the eggs were stored.

"Do the city too," said Keiron. "The people there deserve rain after all this time."

The rain that fell in the city was so abundant, it turned the streets into rivers and flooded the ground floors of innumerable buildings. But the populace did not mind. They splashed about it in with glee. The children jumped naked through it, squealing their delight. The old men and women let it pour over their heads. Families and friends stood in little knots on the roofs of their houses, marvelling at the feel of the rain in their hair, on their skin, listening to the musical sound of it banging and tinkling on dishes and buckets, of its

181

gurgle and bubble at their feet. They were bemused and awed, and profoundly grateful to whatever agency had made this happen. Some linked it with the supposed death of the Queen. A few, clinging to some ancient folk memory of Citatha, the goddess, knelt and offered a prayer of thanks to her.

Justus next dripped blood on the Lizard Caverns. "That will surprise my people," he grinned. "Oh, to see their faces when they hear the water gushing into the caverns!"

"Won't it wash them out, though?" Cassie asked.

"That won't matter now," said Justus, his eyes bright with hope. "We shan't need to hide in there any more. Before long, the whole island will be ours again."

Methodically, Justus pricked his fingers on the lizard and dripped his blood over the map of the whole island. He bore with the discomfort in his hand, and kept at it until the whole Shield was covered with a gleaming film of his amber, translucent blood.

"Now the whole island is blessed with rain," he observed with a profound sigh. "It will seep down into the sand, to the seeds that have patiently waited there for so long – the desert will disappear beneath a carpet of shoots and leaves and flowers and plants of every kind."

"Just as it used to be before the Catastrophe," said Tancred smiling with pleasure.

In the night, Will crept up to the glowing Shield and was startled to see – or think he saw, for he didn't stay long enough to check it – the emerald eye of the Shield's lizard slowly blink.

* * *

Until the rain drained deeper into the sand, it was not safe for them to venture out, for fear they would meet the same fate as the monsters. And so for the next few days they were content to rest, sitting on the parapet in the sun or in the entrance listening to the warm and gentle rain. They watched in delight as the seeds that had lain dormant for generations now at last germinated, sending up shoots with extraordinary rapidity. First there was a carpet of tiny green leaves, growing almost visibly before their eyes. Stems reached up, leaves multiplied. Soon there were plants of all kinds, some instantly flowering, others climbing or spreading great waxy leaves. The speed of the growth was incredible.

Then they heard the croaking of frogs and saw a sudden abundance of them burrowing up through the sand and popping out, their eyes large and incurious, their multi-coloured bodies glistening. The twins – finding the sand near the caves was just firm enough for them to tread on – could not resist picking them up, stroking and tickling them, trying to make instant pets of their favourites. Keiron set Will on the back of one bright red and green frog and it was, as he said with some amusement later, "love at first sight" – the frog and the manikin became inseparable. Even Lord Tancred got caught up in the enthusiasm, allowing the frogs to jump over him as he sat on the rocks, later drawing some of them in his notebook and noting their salient characteristics.

The frogs were followed by bloated and warty toads and little newt-like creatures. The night became full of their incessant croakings.

Keiron and his father took an interest in the camels too. They led them out of their cave into the rain to get a good wash, then brushed them down and fed them as well as they could. The creatures remained lugubrious and indifferent, forever working their lower jaw, in a circular chewing motion or baring their stained teeth, but father and son grew fond of them.

Those lazy days in the Cave Dwellings were like a little holiday, something all of them needed.

One morning Justus announced that, as the sand was at last firm enough to travel on, he was going to the ruined city. He sensed that the lizard-people had left the Lizard Caverns and were gathering there to watch the birth of their young. As their designated leader, he had to be there too, to witness the great moment, the regeneration of their race; he sensed his people calling to him to come.

Tancred said they would follow him on the camels.

Justus did not delay for farewells. He suddenly slithered off at an incredible speed through the new growth, delighting in the wet shade of the leaves and the gentle rain falling on his skin. Every now and then he paused and rose on his hind legs to marvel at the transformation of the island. Where once there had been vast stretches of barren sand and rock, with dusty scrub here and there, over which a roasting wind blew, now all was like a cool, unfolding garden.

Badrur, riding on the neck of his Great Salamander, appeared on the horizon soon after Justus's departure. He too had been delayed by the treachery of the sand.

He had been amazed at the onset of the rain and by the life that was springing up all around him. He was affected less by its beauty, or by its symbolic power, than by the realization that the island – *his* island – was transforming itself into something infinitely desirable: no longer a barren wasteland with one baking city, a few harbour villages and dusty oases, with the inhabitants struggling everywhere to survive in a perpetual drought, but a place full of natural riches. Assuming, that is, that the rains continued.

This could only have come from the magic of the Shield, he concluded; it was inconceivable that it had occurred by chance. Which meant that the Shield wasn't buried in the rubble, as he had thought, but it had been discovered. By whom? And who had unlocked its secrets? Tancred and his brats! Who else? They must have escaped the collapse of the palace. Down the tunnel! Of course! And more than likely with the Shield!

That spurred him on. They could still be at the caves.

He approached the Cave Dwellings from the rear so as not to be seen.

It puzzled him for a while that none of his monsters were there to greet him, even though he had called for them, through the Great Salamander, to meet him – until he guessed the awful truth. He allowed himself some moments of regret: he had become fond of them in his way and they had given him extra power, extra prestige.

But the Great Salamander was more affected. For a

while it swayed its long neck back and forth, making a strange keening noise, and there was nothing Badrur could do to stop it. *I am the last of my kind*, it protested mournfully. *I knew them all. I was their leader. Now I am alone.*

This rather startled Badrur. *You have me*, he said.

We have each other, the Salamander replied dolefully. *That is all.*

That should be enough for you.

The Great Salamander didn't answer. He bowed his head, closed his eyes, and swayed rhythmically, keening again. Badrur had to stand to one side, fuming with impatience, until the creature had mourned enough for the present – not even his hypnotic power could prevent it, which surprised him.

At last he was allowed to climb back on the giant lizard's neck. They moved stealthily around to the front of the caves, keeping low, until Badrur was level with the cave entrance.

The twins and their father were sitting on the parapet, quite unsuspecting about what was going to happen. Unfortunately for them, they had the Shield with them.

The Great Salamander lifted itself on to its hind legs.

It was as if Badrur rose out of nowhere, like an evil spirit out of a a fissure in the earth. The twins screamed.

"I'll take that," Badrur said, his dark eyes gleaming with avarice. *Seize it!* he commanded the Salamander.

The creature lunged at the Shield. Cassie screamed again. Keiron and her father both leapt towards the Shield too. Lord Tancred was knocked to one side by a blow from the Salamander, and Keiron fell flat to avoid the same fate. The Shield clattered to the ground.

Badrur leaned forward and snatched it up. Keiron lunged at it, but just missed. The prince slipped it on his arm and held it up triumphantly.

"It is mine, now, as it always should have been," he shouted at them, and he waved the Shield in front of them, goading them with his triumph.

"It doesn't belong to you, to us, to anyone," Cassie shouted at him, furious. "It belongs to the goddess."

"Huh!" was all he said to that. "This is *my* island, not hers. With my mother dead, I rule here. And what's here is mine."

Tancred struggled to his feet. "Where are you taking it?" he said.

Badrur shrugged. "Back to the city, of course. When the people see the Shield, and know that it brings the rain that they all depend on, they will build me another palace out of the ruins. The scorpion-guards will come back to serve me; and I shall rule over a magnificent new island. I shall be even more powerful even than my mother."

Badrur's loud and mirthless laugh echoed off the cliff.

CHAPTER 12

In anger and despair, they watched the silhouette of Badrur and the Great Salamander slowly recede into the falling twilight. It had all happened so quickly, so unexpectedly, it took a while for it to sink in: *they had lost the Shield*. And lost it to their greatest enemy.

"I should have known he would come," Tancred said bitterly, blaming himself. "Nothing will kill him, he's indestructible. Cities may fall and deserts turn to quicksand, but he will always be there, riding his monster."

"Hush, Father," said Cassie, putting her arm round him. She felt him trembling with emotion.

"At least he didn't think to set his monster on us," Keiron said. "I suppose, as he got what he wanted, we're nothing to him now."

"Of that we should be grateful," Tancred smiled ruefully.

Keiron shielded his eyes against the blood-red light of the sinking sun and said, "Why is he going *that* way? He's not heading back to the city like he said."

Tancred took his notebook from his pocket and unfolded a sketch map of the island tucked inside it.

"It looks like he's going east of the ruined city. The only destination on that route is an oasis to the north-east. Now why would he want to go there?"

They puzzled over that for a while until Will said to Keiron, *He's like a bare tree without a leaf. No one would nest in him.*

Meaning?

Such a tree would like to have poisoned leaves and flowers that sting!

Sting! You mean...? Will, you're a genius!

"Will thinks he going there to make contact with the scorpions," Keiron declared. "Without them, he wouldn't be able to bully the city people into accepting him as their ruler, would he? They'd take the Shield for themselves."

"Of course!" said Tancred. He turned to his children with a sudden look of hope. "Then there's still a chance. If we can get to the lizard-people in time, they can try and stop him. Sooner or later anyway there's going to be a trial of strength with the scorpions; it might as well be now. Come on. If you're up to it, we'll travel in the cool of the night."

The camels were loaded with their few belongings.

The great beasts swayed along at their own leisurely pace. The moon rose slowly in a clear, cold sky and a breeze made the travellers shiver at times. The twins marvelled at the changes in the vast, moonlit landscape, now covered with plants and flowers, huge, arching leaves stretching away on all sides, frogs and lizards plopping and croaking as they passed. Will yearned to see a tree that wasn't a palm, and he noticed with his sharp green eyes shoots that would, in time, stretch up into the sky, creating the warm shade of a forest.

In the early hours of the morning they managed to get a little sleep, stretched out on matting they had brought with them from the caves; but when the rain began to patter down again in great, warm drops, splashing on their skin, they set off once more, chewing as they went such provisions as they had been able to bring with them.

"What do you want to happen, Father?" Keiron asked.

"Here, you mean? Well, the island was once the kingdom of the lizard-people. I believe it should be theirs again."

"But Badrur has a claim, hasn't he?"

"Yes, I can't deny that. But now they are about to ascend again, take what is theirs by right, I feel sure of it. In Justus, I believe, they will have a good leader, despite his youth."

"And the people in the city? The travellers? The fishers? Don't they have a say?"

"Of course they do. I expect they will set up their own administration. I would be surprised if Justus would want to interfere with them. If I judge him right, he won't simply want to replace the Queen, he'll want to live peacefully with everyone here. There won't be any more palaces and bullying guards and summary deaths. I have faith in Justus."

Cassie nodded; she felt the same. "But Tornius would have thought differently," she added.

"You think so?"

"Yes. Sometimes he had the same look in his eye that the Queen had."

"What look?" Keiron asked.

"A look which says: *I always get what I want, no one stands in my way.* Badrur has that look most of all."

The once dusty, ruined, baking city of bare sandstone was now like a hanging garden, with fresh green tendrils and flowers trailing over the remains of the buildings. The rain had washed away much of the sand, so that pitted and cracked roads and steps and broken walls were revealed. The city was full of lizard-people. Having thankfully abandoned the Lizard Caves, they had taken up residence in the ruined houses, swept them of sand to make space. It was perfect for them, providing shelter from the heat and freedom of movement. They were digging big dips in the ground too, to create artificial pools of water in which to splash.

Many of them followed the three travellers on their camels to the great dome in the city centre. There they were welcomed by Justus. He did not rush out to greet them, however, as he would have done a few days before. Now they had to be taken into his presence: they were aware of the significance of that. They were led into the cracked dome which had been cleared of sand. Lizard-people stood or crouched all around the edge. Justus sat on the well, now covered over, with some of the lizard-elders around him. Over the vast floor of the hall were the lizard eggs, large, white and full of cracks. The eggs glistened with rain that dripped from the many fissures in the ceiling.

There was an extraordinary hush in the hall.

Justus jumped down from his place on the well and greeted them, his eyes shining with pleasure. "You're just in time," he whispered solemnly. "The young are about to hatch. The rain has seeped through their shells and has signalled to them that it is time."

They sat around the base of the well. Tancred gave it a rueful look, recalling how he had fallen down it, concussing himself. But the words around its rim had proved both crucial and prophetic: all events have their purpose, he thought.

Justus settled himself between the twins and took their hands. He gave Will, who was standing in Keiron's hair, tense with excitement at what was about to happen, a quick smile of welcome. "I hoped you would all be here to see this," he said.

"Have they made you leader already, then?" Keiron whispered, knowing the answer but wanting to hear what had happened.

"Yes, as soon as I arrived and told them how the rain came, they said my leadership should be confirmed here in this dome. But I can't tell you about the ceremonies, they are secret."

"Congratulations," Cassie whispered, pressing his hand.

There was a sudden rustle and hiss in the hall. Lizard-people leapt on to their hind legs. Justus stood up too.

One egg wobbled. They all gazed at it. Cracks appeared in it, growing bigger by the minute. A bit of shell broke loose; the membrane beneath it trembled and bulged. Then a little wet green snout poked through it. It stayed there for a while, twitching, then disappeared.

There was no other sound or movement in the hall; the suspense was terrific.

The snout appeared again. More shell broke away. Then the baby lizard's head burst through. It looked round, blinking away the thick film on its eye.

The lizard-elders gave orders that the hatching egg should be brought over to Justus. A lizard-woman carefully picked her way through the eggs, several of which were also now wobbling and cracking, and lifted it with reverential care. She presented it to Justus, a huge smile on her face.

He held it out proudly before him. Now the twins and Will could see every movement of the little lizard as it struggled to break free. First one hand came through the shell, then another, pushing away a large fragment.

"It's beautiful," Cassie whispered, wanting to help it hatch.

Keiron was struck by how human the face looked, its eyes a dark green, its face smooth.

The shell split, it fell away, and the baby lizard was revealed, perfect in every detail. It raised itself on its tiny hindlegs and surveyed all those who were watching its birth with such rapt attention. Then it let out a little cry, half-helpless, half-triumphant.

Justus raised the baby lizard above his head as if presenting it symbolically to his people. They responded with cheers and hissings and a great rhythmic thumping of their tails. The twins clapped, and Will jumped up and down on Keiron's head, cheering too.

Tancred murmured congratulations to the lizard-elders, who alone remained composed and grave. "Your forebears had great foresight," he said.

The next few hours were for the twins an extraordinary mixture of fun, excitement, suspense and emotion. Everywhere, shells cracked open and baby lizards wriggled out. Once free, they began to slither about haphazardly, pausing to sniff the air.

"What are they doing?" Cassie asked.

"They are instinctively looking for the lizard who will bring them up," Justus explained.

"Don't you choose them?"

"No, they choose their own parents. For the first few weeks, each baby will have one parent. Once it can survive on its own, it becomes the responsibility of everyone. So this is a great moment. Look, see how my people stand around, none moving: they are waiting to be chosen."

Once a baby lizard touched a lizard-person, it was swept up and cradled, crooned over and licked. It was shown proudly to the others.

By the end of the day, the floor was littered with broken shells. Every hatchling had found a parent.

"That was incredible," Cassie sighed. In fact, she did not think she had witnessed anything more moving.

"Amazing," Keiron echoed. He wished he could adopt a baby lizard for himself.

"We should go now," said Justus. He seemed to radiate happiness. He turned to Lord Tancred. "We need to talk of the Shield."

While this was happening, events to the north of the island were unfolding that would, once again, threaten the lizard-people's very existence.

The Queen's scorpion-guards had retreated to a

distant oasis. They were confused and alarmed. With the Queen's apparent death in the rubble, the centre of their world – literally – had disappeared. They no longer knew what they should do or even what they were for. They squabbled endlessly amongst themselves, which often led to blows and the shedding of blood.

The rain made them feel helpless, too. It mocked all those servile years they had spent guarding the Sacred Spring and rationing its water. It destroyed for them the last shreds of the Queen's authority, dashing hopes that if she was still alive, things might return to normal.

Badrur found them surly and demoralized; but they perked up when they learnt that he had come to save them from their confusion. They all bowed instinctively before him and the Shield, grateful that he had come.

Standing in front of a great seething mass of them, he said, "We shall rebuild the palace and you shall serve me there as you served my mother. But there will be no more guarding of the Sacred Spring – it is sacred no more. You will be there to remind the people of the city the allegiance they owe to me and the Shield. They must be told again and again by you, at every opportunity, that if the Shield should ever be parted from me, the rains will stop and the island will burn up again. Together, we shall be masters of East Island again."

The scorpion-guards whirred their wings, clapped their claws, thumped their shells on the ground in savage delight. Badrur was their saviour and they would serve him to the death as they had served his mother.

Badrur held up his hand for silence. "But there is one great obstacle in our path," he went on. "The lizard-people."

The scorpions hissed their hostility.

"They will multiply now. Swarms of them! We must cut them down before they become too numerous. Most of them are at the ruined city. We must attack them there, now, while they are still weak. This is our chance to kill them once and for all."

The ground-based scorpions fell into lines and began to march, while the airborne ones flew above them. Badrur, riding the Great Salamander, led them out into the desert, with death in their jubilant hearts.

A lizard-guard raced in from an outpost.

"They're coming," he gasped to Justus. "The scorpions. A great swarm of them. And Badrur is leading them on the great beast. They're going to attack us."

Justus shuddered. So soon! They were not sufficiently strong in numbers to tackle this challenge. He went into conclave with the elders and Lord Tancred.

Cassie and Keiron hurried up to the parapet around the roof of the dome, to scan the horizon for first signs of the scorpion army.

"I'm scared," said Cassie. "Especially for Justus and the baby lizards. And if the lizard-people lose, how shall we escape?"

Keiron felt dismal about their prospects too. It was clear that the lizard-people would be outnumbered. Badrur would surely have them killed this time.

What do you think, Will?

The manikin thought for a moment and then said, *I think the lizard-people should be like that cunning creature, the chameleon. I saw one in the palace gardens once. It's a master of camouflage – and it has a deadly tongue*

Deadly? How?

Will explained. Keiron repeated it to Cassie. It was such a devastatingly simple idea, they raced excitedly to the room where the conclave was being held and demanded to see their father.

He took their idea back to Justus and the elders.

Justus came out a little later. "We shall be like our cousins the chameleons," he said with a grin. "It's a brilliant idea."

"Will's idea, really."

"He gets in everywhere, doesn't he," Justus laughed, and to Will's embarrassment, he picked him up and gave him a a lizard-kiss.

The lizard-people hid themselves carefully under leaves over the wide approaches to the ruined city. They listened to the gentle rain patter on the leaves above them. They waited for the enemy, tense, patient and determined.

From the dome's parapet Justus, the twins, Tancred and the Elders kept watch.

"They are perfectly hidden," said Justus. "Using the camouflage just as a chameleon does."

"As long as you keep the benefit of surprise," said Tancred, "you will have the advantage."

At noon, the army of scorpions arrived. Some flew ahead, returning to report that the city seemed deserted. Badrur assumed that the lizard-people had already left. He held up the Shield; it flashed great beams of dazzling sunlight. He urged his army forward.

The scorpion army fell right into the trap: the lizard-people blended in with their surroundings so successfully that the scorpions penetrated to the edge of the city before they even realized the danger.

Justus insisted on joining his people below in this first test of his strength as leader. He was one of the first to hurl his venom: it hit a scorpion directly in the eyes, causing almost instant death. Camouflaged in the leaves, hurling their venom – just as the chameleon darts out its long, sticky tongue to catch the unwary fly – the lizard-people scored hit after deadly hit. As soon as they had made their strike, they melted back into the cover of the leaves. It was so devastatingly effective, they sustained few casualties themselves.

The twins, Tancred and Will watched from the dome's parapet with some of the lizard-elders. They could see very little, however. Just Badrur on his Great Salamander, hurling ineffective commands, and the flying scorpions hovering helplessly above the battlefield. In a fury, Badrur ordered them down, which was a mistake, as they soon met the same fate as the rest.

The battle – if it can be called that – was swift, deadly, one-sided and horribly effective in its simplicity: a silent rout. At last, conceding defeat, most of the flying scorpions cut their losses and flew away. A few stayed loyal to their leader, buzzing confusedly in the air about the Great Salamander's head. Some of the ground-based scorpions managed to break away too, but not many.

Badrur, barely unable to believe the swift calamity that had befallen him, ordered the Great Salamander to retreat. The Shield now dangled on a strap at his side.

As soon as they saw the great beast turn, the lizard-people emerged from their hiding places and swarmed across the ground to intercept the prince and his mount. Suddenly, Badrur was in the midst of a sea of lizard-people. The Great Salamander was forced to stop.

"Trample on them!" Badrur ordered.

The Great Salamander swayed its head on its long neck from side to side, agitated and uncertain.

"Crush them!" Badrur shouted, digging his heels hard into the creature's muscles and tugging furiously on its ruff.

Justus raised himself on his hind legs in front of the Great Salamander. "Listen to me," he shouted at the creature. "We are all of one kind. Lizards! From the same ancient family."

"Kill him," Badrur screamed. He bent forward and tried to fix the Great Salamander with his hypnotic eye, but the beast tossed its great head. *Do as I say or I will kill you too*, Badrur shouted. Those words shuddered through the great beast; it was already feeling sore and disorientated by the death of its fellow monsters, and by the awful, lonely fact that it was now unique in the world, and these words were like salt on a wound. Rebellion flared in its mind.

"Listen!" Justus said to the beast, looking into its dark and confused eye. "You are not our real enemy. You are a lizard, like all of us. You might have been king of this land, all those years ago. Think of it: you might even have sired us all! You may be our Great Father. Have you never thought of that?"

"He is speaking rubbish," Badrur shouted, trying to tug the Great Salamander away.

But that only made the beast more stubborn. What Justus had said appealed to it, perhaps touching some deep, inchoate memory. The creature lifted its old head and cast its gaze over the field of watching lizard-people. Some deep recognition took hold in its mind, and the more Badrur shouted and insulted, the more it clung to the idea.

"You have become Badrur's slave," Justus shouted, seeing that his words were having an effect. "Is that what you want to be?"

The beast growled.

"Throw him off," Justus shouted. "Be one of us."

Be one of us. That was the sentence that finally broke Badrur's hold over its mind. The words dispersed the last of the hypnotic fog in its mind and gave it back its will. It bellowed, a great deep sound that made the lizard-people shiver: it was like a cry from their souls for all that their race had suffered under the yoke of the Queen, her forebears and descendant.

It reared up, shook its head vigorously, and kept on shaking. Badrur, clinging ever more precariously to its ruff, was finally thrown clear. He sprawled ignominiously in the sand, scorpions buzzing around him.

The Great Salamander gave a last great bellow, a mixture of triumph and pain, and lumbered off, desperate to get away from them all, hungry for the freedom that awaited it in the flourishing land. Out there it would think about its relationship with the lizard-people; and in time, they would look after it.

The Shield had been shaken free too. It lay glinting in the wet sand among dripping and trampled leaves. Justus seized it. He brushed the sand away and held it up for all to see. It was a sign that their battle had been victorious, and it set the seal on his leadership. He turned the Shield to face the dome where he knew the twins and the elders were watching.

The lizard-people swarmed around him, lifted him up and carried him back towards the ruined city in one excited, happy mass.

"Look!" Keiron exclaimed.

"I am looking," said Cassie, her eyes fixed on Justus's slow progress.

"No, over there. Badrur! He's getting away."

She saw several flying scorpions lift the prince out of a mêlée of lizard-people and flying venom. Several scorpions were hit, but enough remained airborne to carry Badrur up and away. The last the twins and Tancred saw of him on East Island was as a dark speck flying off into the heart of the sun.

Badrur was still being carried, half-conscious from the fierce heat, from lack of water, and poisoned with bitterness, when the Child, still at the Spring with the now imbecilic Queen, looked up and saw him fly over. A yearning for him made her cry out and start up. She picked up the Queen, as if the frail old lady was no more than a rag-doll, and set off in the direction the flying party had taken. The dark magnetism that existed between the prince and the Child, attracting and repelling, made her journey inevitable. She was comforted by the garbled nursery songs the Queen sang as they pounded through the bright green leaves, dripping with rain.

"What will you do now, Justus?" Keiron asked.

They had spent some days helping the baby lizards explore their new world.

"We shall rebuild this ancient city," he said. "This is where we shall live, though I'm sure my people will gradually spread all over the island again. And you," he added, with evident reluctance, "it is time for you to leave, too."

"We know," said Cassie. "But I'm sure we'll come back and see you. The island's a beautiful place now."

And indeed it was; it promised to be a paradise.

"You are aware, Justus, that at last the Shield's work is done?" Tancred observed. "The rain will always fall now, it is not dependent on your blood or the presence of the Shield on this island."

Justus nodded. "I feel it in my bones," he said. "And the Elders think so, too."

"You know that the goddess wants the Shield?"

"Then she shall have it."

The long, meandering journey south on camels to the harbour was a pleasant one. The intermittent rain kept the twins and their father relatively cool and there was much to see. Justus and a group of lizard-people accompanied them. They passed the outskirts of the city and could see, from a vantage point on a hill, the people clearing the palace gardens of the rubble.

"Look," cried Cassie. "The palace fountains are flowing again."

The ship was as they had left it moored in the harbour.

They dismounted at the quay, said fond farewells to their lugubrious camels, waved to the lizard-people and assembled crowds, and rowed out to the ship.

Justus swam by the boat's side. "I won't come on deck," he said, when they arrived. "I'll watch from here."

"Oh, please come!" Keiron pleaded; he wanted to delay their farewell to Justus until the last possible minute. But the lizard-boy shook his head.

Once on deck, Tancred unwrapped the Shield from its protective covering and handed it to Cassie. "Your turn, I believe," he said with an encouraging smile.

They climbed to the bridge.

"Here goes, then," said Cassie, taking a deep breath.

She held the Shield up to face the sun. A great beam of light was reflected from it.

She closed her eyes, the better to concentrate, and thought of the goddess's disembodied voice in the vault on Temple Island. Keiron thought of the Golden Armour, lying there waiting for the Shield.

Tancred watched his children proudly.

The light swirled around them. A moment before it sealed them off from the outside world, the twins turned and waved to Justus bobbing in the water below them, and he waved back for the last time. How hard it was to say goodbye!

The light became a golden tunnel. It arched like a rainbow over the sea.

The ship shifted, rose slowly and majestically, and floated into the tunnel of light.

The twins and Lord Tancred had secured the Golden Helmet for the goddess – and now the Golden Shield. More terrifying quests awaited them in the months ahead – they all dimly knew that – but only Will, with prophetic glimpses into the future, had any idea what shape they would take, and he wasn't telling. He settled back in Keiron's hair and let the golden light flow over him.

Have you read the
first book in the series?

THE HELMET

Tara the wolf-girl stood in the shelter of an oak tree and shivered. The cold wind buffeted the tree-tops and crept icily through the undergrowth. In the forest clearing, the wolf-people had arrived back home, having served for a month as servants in the Mansion. They were milling about excitedly, yapping, licking, nipping, barking, rolling about in the leaves together. Tara watched them, sad and yearning.

Mingling with the welcomes were loud and tearful farewells. Those who were going back to the Mansion, as replacement servants, slipped regretfully out of their skins, and stood naked and shivering as humans in the frosty moonlight. The new arrivals seized their discarded skins and wriggled into them, a look of profound relief on their wolfish faces.

Tara had heard many stories of the Mansion, of the ways of humans, of their peculiar smell and lack of fur, of their cunning and mastery. One of the humans was now visible above the commotion. Aulic. He was standing on a sledge, wrapped in a great black bear-skin, waving his arms about, shouting.

She watched restlessly, softly yapping to herself. Circling the edge of the clearing, and averting her eyes from the scenes of reunion, she paused behind a log and watched Aulic. How ugly he was, how powerful; he struck an obscure terror in her. But humans fascinated her. She had watched them hunting and trapping: they seemed so slow and helpless on their two legs, and yet so dangerous.

Stepping from behind the log, she paused at the edge of the clearing, wondering what she should do. Naked wolf-people were clambering on to the carts and sledges, huddling together under deer- and bear-skins.

She had been told of the children of the Mansion, of Keiron and Cassie: two exalted human children with no mother and an eccentric father. She had heard how Cassie had often been there to welcome the new batch of wolf-servants, to warm them with kind words and see that they were settled in; and of how Keiron would show them through all the dark and twisting passages of the great house.

Aulic gracelessly accepted a horn of water from a wolf-woman, and gulped down the cold, brackish liquid. He flung the horn aside, swore at any wolf-person in sight and shouted at the more timid stragglers: "Get a move on. I'm not waiting any longer."

For some time now, Tara had had an obscure sense that she stood apart from her pack. Was she the only one who was reluctant to return to her wolf-skin? Who sometimes found her human form more beautiful than her wolf one? Often, she yearned to strike out into the dark forest on her own. But where would she go?

As she watched the wolf-people huddling under the furs on the giant sledges, ready to set out for the Mansion, an impulse rose up in her, a crackle of energy that made her leap up and yelp. She was much too young to serve in the Mansion, but that wasn't going to stop her now. She raced over the clearing towards the nearest sledge, even as Aulic was signalling for them to leave.

Tara heard voices behind her, calling her back, but she did not heed them. With one concentrated twist of her body, she shed her skin. She felt a pang of remorse as it slid to her feet, but she knew that it would be well looked after in her absence. Not pausing to look at her moon-white human form, she clambered on to the nearest sledge and slid under a pile of furs.

"It's not your turn, girl," voices among the furs said. "You're too young." But it was too late, whips were being cracked, horses were snorting, sledges were turning: they were on the move.

An hour later, they emerged from the wind-torn forest and struck out over rugged brush. Here the full force of the wind hit them, threatening to snatch away their mounds of furs. The horses struggled on, their heads bent, goaded by the sting of whips. Tara felt the cold envelop her; she pulled the dead skins tighter around her, realizing the mad sacrifice she had made in leaving her own skin behind.

At last they came to the top of a high, flat ridge, where the horses were allowed to catch their breath. Far away in the distance a cold, metallic sea glittered fitfully in the moonlight between scudding clouds. Below them, on the rocky coast, stood the Mansion, a sprawling, shadowy building, surrounded by outbuildings and a circling wall. Faint lights flickered in many windows.

They trotted the last stretch down to the house, the horses breathing heavily after their long trek.

The great gates of the Mansion opened to swallow them up. The wolf-people emerged from their sledges, blinking and apprehensive, jostling together uncertainly in a dank courtyard. No stories of the Mansion ever prepared them for the first shock of that dark and gloomy place of shadows.

Tara was in panic at being hemmed in and surrounded by looming walls and turrets. She hid behind a rotting water-butt against a wall. She heard Aulic telling them to enter the Mansion at once. She wanted to join them, but she felt paralysed with a nameless fear. She curled her strange, elongated body into a tight ball, wishing for her wolf-tail that it might cover her eyes.

After what seemed an endless time, she felt a warm hand on her arm and heard a soft, coaxing voice. She shrank back and opened her eyes.

A few minutes earlier, Cassie, the daughter of the Mansion, twelve years old, opened a window that overlooked the courtyard and leaned on the sill. She watched the wolf-people slip out from under the mounds of furs on the carts and hurry, suspicious and a little afraid, into the building. How ridiculous Aulic looked in that oversized coat!

The wind whipped her long, thick, ash-blonde hair into her eyes; parting it, she caught sight of the wolf-girl still huddled behind the water-butt. She craned to get a better view and saw, even from this distance, that the wolf-girl was trembling. Poor thing! And what was one so young doing here, anyway?

She ran down the stone stairs and hurried into the courtyard, just missing bumping into Aulic who was waddling determinedly across the flagstones towards the wolf-girl.

"Out!" he shouted at Tara, and when she did not immediately respond, he began to prod her. "Come on, out!"

"Let me talk to her," said Cassie. She pushed the man-servant aside.

She crouched beside Tara and said, "Don't be afraid. What is the matter?"

Tara looked into the girl's brown eyes and beautiful face and at once felt her trembling ease. She tried to answer but, although she had been taught from infancy to speak the human tongue, what came out was a sort of strangled yelp.

Cassie spoke soothingly to her and soon coaxed her out.

"Inside," Aulic ordered impatiently, grasping the wolf-girl's arm to propel her forward.

Cassie detested the lack of respect he always showed towards the wolf-people, and her anger flared. "I'm taking this one, Aulic," she said, and she pushed his hand away.

"Now, then, Miss Cassie," he growled. He had never liked the child and at times found it hard to hide the fact.

"It's lucky that she's come at this time," Cassie answered. "I was looking for a maid for myself, you know. *A personal* one."

Aulic scowled.

"Come on," said Cassie gently to Tara. "Follow me." She swept past Aulic, hiding her grin behind her haughtiness, pulling Tara along with her.

Tara took a while to get used to being inside a building, especially one so dark and sprawling, full of closed doors and receding passages.

They sat side by side, shyly at first, on Cassie's bed,

and Tara told of her impetuous leap on to the cart in the wood, and of the feeling that somehow she did not quite belong to her pack. Under Cassie's careful probing, she revealed something of what it was like to be a young wolf, learning to blend in with the pack, to use foliage as camouflage, to track down game, to listen for signs of danger...

In turn, Cassie described her life in the Mansion with her father, Lord Tancred, and her twin brother Keiron. Her father, she said, was a mage and scholar, far more interested in things found in books and scrolls or maps of the heavens than in the life around him, but she and her brother loved him, for all his eccentricities. They spent their day studying, reading stories, playing shuttlecock, roaming in the woods nearby when the weather wasn't too bad, and talking to their father in the evening when he took his mind off his books.

Tara noticed that Cassie made no mention of her mother. Not being close to her own parents – wolf-people merge into the pack from an early age – she did not hesitate to ask about her.

"I don't know," Cassie mumbled, shaking her head slightly and looking away. "Father won't tell us."

"Why not?"

She shrugged. "He likes mysteries, I suppose." She smiled ironically, then took a deep breath. "No, that's not it. I think something happened to my mother when Keiron and I were infants. Father says she didn't die, exactly, she just, well, changed." The subject confused her and she found it hard to talk about.

"Like we do, you mean?" Tara said brightly. "Change from wolf into human and back again."

Cassie considered this. "Perhaps that's it. Although, if she can change back into human, why have we never seen her?" She fell silent.

The wolf-girl was fascinated by the tall mirror in Cassie's bedroom. She shied away from her reflection at first, then touched it in puzzlement – it was so much clearer than anything she had seen in water. Growing bolder, she tried to reach her image by looking behind the mirror. Her bewilderment, her wonder, delighted Cassie.

For the rest of the day Tara tried on Cassie's clothes, shrieking and laughing at the sight of herself in them; and then they wandered around the Mansion. But Cassie didn't at first introduce her to Keiron and her father: she was too pleased to have the wolf-girl all to herself.

"I'm so glad I caught sight of you behind that water-butt," Cassie said. "If I hadn't, you'd be down in the wolf-quarters with all the others and I might never have noticed you."

Tara smiled. "I feel ashamed of the fear I felt," she said.

"Well, you've nothing to fear now. And don't take any notice of Aulic. He likes to bully the wolf-people, but if he ever tries it with you, you just let me know."

"Thank you," Tara murmured. She slipped her arm through Cassie's.

"You won't mind being separated from the other wolf-people," Cassie asked, "to be up here with me?"

There was a glint of happiness in Tara's slanted eyes

which Cassie could not mistake. "I shall love it here," the wolf-girl said.

She slept on a large cushion at the foot of Cassie's bed, curling up as if she was still a wolf, and sometimes Cassie would hear her yelping softly in her sleep, as if she was still running with the pack.

While Cassie had been making friends with Tara, Keiron had been in his room, sprawled against the base of his bed with his bare feet toasting before the fire. There was a large, old leather-bound book on his lap, full of his favourite stories written out in a careful calligraphy. He wondered vaguely what was keeping his sister; probably chatting with the new wolf-people, he thought, turning the page. He knew he should be helping to show the new wolf-people around the Mansion, but he could not tear himself away from the book and the fire.

He was reading one of the many legends about the Golden Armour. There was a picture of the Armour opposite the story, lying on a slab of rock in the temple vault, its golden gloves folded on its breastplate, a glow emanating from it in the mysterious gloom. Such pictures always stirred something deep, nervous and dangerous in his imagination, as if for a moment he had caught a glimpse of another reality far more exciting than his own.

One story he particularly liked told of an exiled king who landed on Temple Island with his grown-up son and found the Golden Armour in the ruins of the temple. The goddess Citatha asked him to take the Helmet, the Shield, the Spurs and the Sword and place one of each on the four main islands. "They hold my magic," she said. "Whoever can unlock it will transform these islands into a paradise, where I may rule again."

The king did as she asked, keeping the Helmet for North Island where he settled. He built a castle on the northernmost tip of the island, and waited for the Helmet to work its magic. But nothing happened!

Keiron wondered what came first, the story or the castle. There was a teasing quality about these stories which unsettled him: were they history or fantasy?

He turned the page and came across a picture of the king's son, a tall, handsome youth with blazing, hypnotic eyes. This prince quarrelled with his father, he read, and fled to East Island. There, he found hideous monsters which he hypnotized and mastered. He built a great dome to house the Golden Shield; but, like his father with the Helmet, he could not work its magic: Keiron delighted in the numerous attempts the prince made, each more original than the last, to unlock the Shield's secret.

Keiron closed the book with a satisfying thump.

He felt a movement in his hair.

Well, Will, he said telepathically, *what did you think of that one?*

In his long, uncombed, flaxen-coloured hair, Will, Keiron's little wooden manikin, stretched and yawned. He was no taller than Keiron's hand.

About a year ago, Keiron had carved him out of a piece of willow he had found in the forest. He had "seen" the shape of the wooden boy in the bark, in the contours of its twigs and knots. Will – as Keiron promptly, if rather unimaginatively, called him – emerged from the wood almost as if the knife was simply peeling back layers of wood fibre to reveal him already there.

Cassie had soon got interested in the manikin. "He looks so real, in a funny sort of way," she observed, studying his face, his glossy green eyes. "If only..."

Then a miraculous thing happened.

She stroked Will, concentrating hard on his inertness, hardly aware of what she was doing; and when she felt the sap agitate within him, she wished that he was alive. Suddenly, he wriggled in her hands. She was so startled she shrieked and dropped him. Will fell to the floor, sat up, looked up at them in bewilderment, then scratched his head and grinned.

When she was still a small child, Cassie had discovered that she could heal little creatures that seemed sick: she'd stroke them and feel some sort of energy flow into them from her fingers; and suddenly, they'd scamper or fly away as right as rain. She did not understand why she had this power, but it was all of a piece with other inexplicable things in nature, and the twins had got used to it.

But she had never brought alive something hand-made before, and she did not know what to make of it.

Now there were three of them. For quite some time, Cassie found it hard to get used to the idea that her brother had someone else to turn to now, someone ever closer to hand than herself; and she was always a little cool and mocking towards Will.

Keiron had a gift too – not such a powerful one, but inexplicable nevertheless. From an early age he had learnt that he could "speak" to things in his head. Wood, stone, pottery, weave, sand, water, mud, whatever – they all had a voice in his head and would answer his questions if they had a mind to. It proved quite a useful gift, too: for instance, if he mislaid things, he could ask where they were, or if he got lost he could ask his way home. Occasionally, too, if he was bored, he might ask something old to tell him its life story, which could be quite amusing.

It was because of this gift that he and Will were able to talk to each other telepathically, and that was the best use he put it to, by a long way.

Well, what did you think of that story? Good, wasn't it? Do you think the Golden Armour really exists? said Will.

Of course I do! And one day, Will – I'll tell you this and no one else – I'm going to find it.

It was meant to be an idle boast, but somehow it came out differently. Like a prophecy echoing from another time. And Keiron shivered.

Cassie brought Tara in to meet her brother. They smiled and nodded at each other shyly. He was fascinated by the wolf-girl's slanting, almond-shaped amber eyes, by the way she put her head to one side on hearing faint sounds far away in the building, by how her nose twitched too as she picked up currents of scent he had no inkling of. She was beautiful, too, in a dark, wild, woody kind of way; her skin was very white and unblemished, her hands were long and thin.

Keiron was a little startled at the closeness that had sprung up between the two girls; normally, since they only spent a month with the wolf-people, there was never enough time to make friends with them. And she was so young. But he felt happy for his sister: he had sensed lately that there were times when she needed a friend besides himself.

For a while Tara was tongue-tied in the boy's presence. She could see the close resemblance between him and his sister – the same texture and colour of hair, the same bright, searching look in their eyes, the same unconscious gestures of friendliness – but it was the differences that struck her. While Cassie was like the dark reflections on a pool in a wood, he reflected the wavering light, his thoughts passing like fish just under the surface: that was her initial impression.

"And this is Will," said Cassie, snatching the inquisitive manikin from Keiron's hair. "He can only speak to Keiron, no one else. Hold him, if you like."

Being both from the forest, Tara and the manikin had their own instinctive language; it was made up of signs and touches, and the twins watched delighted as Tara and Will got to know each other. He ran over her, peered into her ears, got her long silver-brown hair in tangles, slid down her arms and eventually settled on to her lap.

"Here, Cass," said Keiron, picking up the leather-bound book, "I found a new picture of the Golden Helmet."

They all stared at the full-page illustration. Something hypnotic seemed to emanate from it. Tara shivered and turned away, as if a cold draught had passed over her. Will sat on the edge of the page and slowly shook his head.

"It's very handsome," said Cassie. "But the darkness in that visor scares me a bit. I don't know why. Like there should be eyes there, not emptiness."

"I know," said Keiron. "I'd love to put it on, wouldn't you? Oh, Cass, we should look for the Golden Helmet. All the stories say it's here, on North Island. Don't you think?"

Cassie's face brightened, and she opened her mouth to speak.

"I can hear the wolves howling in the wood," Tara interrupted, lifting her head. A look of pain came into her eyes and she turned away.

Cassie felt for Tara's hand. It was cold.

"You don't wish you were with them, do you? You *could* go back if you wish. I could talk to Aulic about it."

Tara shook her head.

"Come on, then," said Keiron, trying to cheer them up. "Let's settle down and hear another story."